Miss Bracegirdle & Other Stories by Stacy Aumonier

Stacy Aumonier was born at Hampstead Road near Regent's Park, London on 31st March 1877.

He came from a family with a strong and sustained tradition in the visual arts; sculptors and painters.

On leaving school it seemed the family tradition would also be his career path. In particular his early talents were that of a landscape painter. He exhibited paintings at the Royal Academy in the early years of the twentieth century.

In 1907 he married the international concert pianist, Gertrude Peppercorn, at West Horsley in Surrey. A year later Aumonier began a career in a second branch of the arts at which he enjoyed a short but outstanding success—as a stage performer writing and performing his own sketches.

The Observer newspaper commented that "...the stage lost in him a real and rare genius, he could walk out alone before any audience, from the simplest to the most sophisticated, and make it laugh or cry at will."

In 1915, Aumonier published a short story 'The Friends' which was well received (and was subsequently voted one of the 15 best stories of 1915 by the Boston Magazine, Transcript).

Despite his age in 1917 at age 40 he was called up for service in World War I. He began as a private in the Army Pay Corps, and then transferred as a draughtsman in the Ministry of National Service.

By now he had four books published—two novels and two books of short stories—and his occupation is recorded with the Army Medical Board as 'author.'

In the mid-1920s, Aumonier received the shattering diagnosis that he had contracted tuberculosis. In the last few years of his life, he would spend long spells in various sanatoria, some better than others.

Shortly before his death, Stacy Aumonier sought treatment in Switzerland, but died of the disease in Clinique La Prairie at Clarens beside Lake Geneva on 21st December 1928. He was 55.

Index of Contents
Miss Bracegirdle Does Her Duty
Where Was Wych Street?
The Octave of Jealously
The Accident of Crime
The Funny Man's Day
Old Fags
Stacy Aumonier - A Short Biography
Stacy Aumonier - A Concise Bibliography

D1594484

Miss Bracegirdle Does Her Duty

"This is the room, madame."

"Ah, thank you—thank you."

"Does it appear satisfactory to madame?"

"Oh, yes. Thank you—quite."

"Does madame require anything further?"

"Er—if not too late, may I have a hot bath?"

"Parfaitement, madame. The bathroom is at the end of the passage on the left. I will go and prepare it for madame."

"There is one thing more. I have had a very long journey. I am very tired. Will you please see that I am not disturbed in the morning until I ring?"

"Certainly, madame."

Millicent Bracegirdle was speaking the truth—she was tired. But then, in the sleepy cathedral town of Easing- stoke, from which she came, it was customary for everyone to speak the truth. It was customary, moreover, for everyone to lead simple, self-denying lives—to give up their time to good works and elevating thoughts. One had only to glance at little Miss Bracegirdle to see that in her were epitomized all the virtues and ideals of Easingstoke. Indeed, it was the pursuit of duty which had brought her to the Hotel de l'Ouest at Bordeaux on this summer's night. She had travelled from Easingstoke to London, then without a break to Dover, crossed that horrid stretch of sea to Calais, entrained for Paris, where of necessity she had to spend four hours—a terrifying experience—and then had come on to Bordeaux, arriving at midnight. The reason of this journey being that someone had to come to Bordeaux to meet her young sister-in-law, who was arriving the next day from South America. The sister-in-law was married to a missionary in Paraguay, but the climate not agreeing with her, she was returning to England. Her dear brother, the dean, would have come himself, but the claims on his time were so extensive, the parishioners would miss him so—it was clearly Millicent's duty to go.

She had never been out of England before, and she had a horror of travel, and an ingrained distrust of foreigners. She spoke a little French, sufficient for the purpose of travel and for obtaining any modest necessities, but not sufficient for carrying on any kind of conversation. She did not deplore this latter fact, for she was of opinion that French people were not the kind of people that one would naturally want to have conversation with; broadly speaking, they were not quite "nice," in spite of their ingratiating manners.

She unpacked her valise, placed her things about the room, tried to thrust back the little stabs of home-sickness as she visualized her darling room at the deanery. How strange and hard and unfriendly seemed these foreign hotel bedrooms! No chintz and lavender and photographs of all the dear family, the dean, the nephews and nieces, the interior of the Cathedral during harvest festival; no samplers and needlework or coloured reproductions of the paintings by Marcus Stone. Oh, dear, how foolish she was! What did she expect?

She disrobed, and donned a dressing-gown; then, armed with a sponge-bag and towel, she crept timidly down the passage to the bathroom, after closing her bedroom door and turning out the light. The gay bathroom cheered her. She wallowed luxuriously in the hot water, regarding her slim legs with quiet satisfaction. And for the first time since leaving home there came to her a pleasant moment, a sense of enjoyment in her adventure. And after all, it was rather an adventure, and her life had been peculiarly devoid of it. What queer lives some people must live, travelling about, having experiences! How old was she? Not really old—not by any means. Forty-two? Forty-three? She had shut herself up so. She hardly ever regarded the potentialities of age. As the world went, she was a well-preserved woman for her age. A life of self-abnegation, simple living, healthy walking, and fresh air had kept her younger than these hurrying, pampered, city people.

Love? Yes, once when she was a young girl—he was a schoolmaster, a most estimable, kind gentleman. They were never engaged—not actually, but it was a kind of understood thing. For three years it went on, this pleasant understanding and friendship. He was so gentle, so distinguished and considerate. She would have been happy to have continued in this strain for ever. But there was something lacking—Stephen had curious restless lapses. From the physical aspect of marriage she shrank—yes, even with Stephen, who was gentleness and kindness itself. And then, one day—one day he went away, vanished, and never returned. They told her he had married one of the country girls, a girl who used to work in Mrs. Forbes's dairy—not a very nice girl, she feared, one of those fast, pretty, foolish women. Heigho! Well, she had lived that down, destructive as the blow appeared at the time. One lives everything down in time. There is always work, living for others, faith, duty. At the same time she could sympathize with people who found satisfaction in unusual experiences.

There would be lots to tell the dear dean when she wrote to him on the morrow: nearly losing her spectacles on the restaurant-car, the amusing remarks of an American child on the train to Paris, the curious food everywhere, nothing simple and plain; the two English ladies at the hotel in Paris who told her about the death of their uncle—the poor man being taken ill on Friday and dying on Sunday afternoon, just before tea-time; the kindness of the hotel proprietor, who had sat up for her; the prettiness of the chambermaid. Oh, yes, everyone was really very kind. The French people, after all, were very nice. She had seen nothing—nothing but what was quite nice and decorous. There would be lots to tell the dean to-morrow.

Her body glowed with the friction of the towel. She again donned her night attire and her thick woolen dressing-gown. She tidied up the bathroom carefully in exactly the same way she was accustomed to do at home; then once more gripped her sponge-bag and towel, and turning out the light she crept down the passage to her room. Entering the room, she switched on the light and shut the door quickly. Then one of those ridiculous things happened, just the kind of thing you would expect to happen in a foreign hotel. The handle of the door came off in her hand. She ejaculated a quiet "Bother!" and sought to replace it with one hand, the other being occupied with the towel and sponge-bag. In doing this she behaved foolishly, for, thrusting the knob carelessly against the steel pin without properly securing it, she only succeeded in pushing the pin farther into the door, and the knob was not adjusted. She uttered another little "Bother!" and put her sponge-bag and towel down on the floor. She then tried to recover the pin with her left hand, but it had gone in too far.

"How very foolish!" she thought. "I shall have to ring for the chambermaid—and perhaps the poor girl has gone to bed."

She turned and faced the room, and suddenly the awful horror was upon her.

There was a man asleep in her bed!

The sight of that swarthy face on the pillow, with its black tousled hair and heavy moustache, produced in her the most terrible moment of her life. Her heart nearly stopped. For some seconds she could neither think nor scream, and her first thought was:—

"I mustn't scream!"

She stood there like one paralysed, staring at the man's head and the great curved hunch of his body under the clothes. When she began to think she thought very quickly and all her thoughts worked together. The first vivid realisation was that it wasn't the man's fault; it was her fault. She was in the wrong room. It was the man's room. The rooms were identical, but there were all his things about, his clothes thrown carelessly over chairs, his collar and tie on the wardrobe, his great heavy boots and the strange yellow trunk. She must get out—somehow, anyhow. She clutched once more at the door, feverishly driving her finger-nails into the hole where the elusive pin had vanished. She tried to force her fingers in the crack and open the door that way, but it was of no avail. She was to all intents and purposes locked in—locked in a bedroom in a strange hotel, alone with a man—a foreigner— a Frenchman!

She must think—she must think! She switched off the light. If the light was off he might not wake up. It might give her time to think how to act. It was surprising that he had not awakened. If he did wake up, what would he do? How could she explain herself? He wouldn't believe her. No one would believe her. In an English hotel it would be difficult enough, but here, where she wasn't known, where they were all foreigners and consequently antagonistic—merciful heavens!

She must get out. Should she wake the man? No, she couldn't do that. He might murder her. He might—oh, it was too awful to contemplate! Should she scream? Ring for the chambermaid? But no; it would be the same thing. People would come rushing. They would find her there in the strange man's bedroom after midnight—she, Millicent Bracegirdle, sister of the Dean of Easingstoke! Easingstoke! Visions of Easingstoke flashed through her alarmed mind. Visions of the news arriving, women whispering around tea tables: "Have you heard, my dear? Really, no one would have imagined! Her poor brother! He will, of course, have to resign, you know, my dear. Have a little more cream, my love."

Would they put her in prison? She might be in the room for the purpose of stealing or she might be in the room for the purpose of breaking every one of the ten commandments. There was no explaining it away. She was a ruined woman, suddenly and irretrievably, unless she could open the door. The chimney? Should she climb up the chimney? But where would that lead to? And then she thought of the man pulling her down by the legs when she was already smothered in soot. Any moment he might wake up. She thought she heard the chambermaid going along the passage. If she had wanted to scream, she ought to have screamed before. The maid would know she had left the bathroom some minutes ago. Was she going to her room?

An abrupt and desperate plan formed in her mind. It was already getting on for one o'clock. The man was probably a quite harmless commercial traveller or business man. He would probably get up about seven or eight o'clock, dress quickly, and go out. She would hide under his bed until he went. Only a matter of a few hours. Men don't look under their beds, although she made a religious practice of doing so herself. When he went he would be sure to open the door all right. The handle would be lying on the floor as though it had dropped off in the night. He would probably ring for the chambermaid, or open it with a pen-knife. Men are so clever at those things. When he had gone she would creep out and steal back to her room, and then there would be no necessity to give any explanation to anyone. But heavens! what an experience! Once under the white frill of that bed, she would be safe till the morning. In daylight nothing seemed so terrifying. With feline precaution she went down on her hands and knees and crept towards the bed. What a lucky thing there was that broad white frill! She lifted it at the foot of the bed and crept under. There was just sufficient depth to take her slim body. The floor was fortunately carpeted all over, but it seemed very close and dusty. Suppose she coughed or sneezed! Anything might happen. Of course, it would be much more difficult to explain her presence under the bed than to explain her presence just inside the door. She held her breath in suspense. No sound came from above, but under the frill it was difficult to hear anything. It was almost more nerve-racking than hearing everything—listening for signs and portents. This temporary escape, in any case, would give her time to regard the predicament detachedly. Up to the present she had not been able to focus the full significance of her action. She had, in truth, lost her head. She had been like a wild animal, consumed with the sole idea of escape—a mouse or a cat would do this kind of thing—take cover and lie low. If only it hadn't all happened abroad!

She tried to frame sentences of explanation in French, but French escaped her. And then they talked so rapidly, these people. They didn't listen. The situation was intolerable. Would she be able to endure a night of it? At present she was not altogether uncomfortable, only stuffy and—very, very frightened. But she had to face six or seven or eight hours of it, and perhaps even then discovery in the end! The minutes flashed by as she turned the matter over and over in her head. There was no solution. She began to wish she had screamed or awakened the man. She saw now that that would have been the wisest and most politic thing to do; but she had allowed ten minutes or a quarter of an hour to elapse from the moment when the chambermaid would know that she had left the bathroom. They would want an explanation of what she had been doing in the man's bedroom all that time. Why hadn't she screamed before?

She lifted the frill an inch or two and listened. She thought she heard the man breathing, but she couldn't be sure. In any case, it gave her more air. She became a little bolder, and thrust her face partly through the frill so that she could breathe freely. She tried to steady her nerves by concentrating on the fact that—well, there it was. She had done it. She must make the best of it. Perhaps it would be all right, after all.

"Of course, I sha'n't sleep," she kept on thinking. "I sha'n't be able to. In any case, it will be safer not to sleep. I must be on the watch."

She set her teeth and waited grimly. Now that she had made up her mind to see the thing through in this manner she felt a little calmer. She almost smiled as she reflected that there would certainly be something to tell the dear dean when she wrote to him to-morrow. How would he take it? Of course he would believe it—he had never doubted a single word that she had uttered in her life—but the story would sound so preposterous. In Easingstoke it would be almost impossible to imagine such an experience. She, Millicent Bracegirdle, spending a night under a strange man's bed in a foreign hotel! What would those women think? Fanny Shields and that garrulous old Mrs. Rusbridger? Perhaps—yes, perhaps it would be advisable to tell the dear dean to let the story go no farther. One could hardly expect Mrs. Rusbridger to not make implications—exaggerate. Oh, dear! what were they all doing now? They would all be asleep, everyone in Easingstoke. Her dear brother always retired at 10.15. He would be sleeping calmly and placidly, the sleep of the just—breathing the clear sweet air of Sussex, not this—oh, it was stuffy! She felt a great desire to cough. She mustn't do that.

Yes, at 9.30 all the servants were summoned to the library. There was a short service—never more than fifteen minutes; her brother didn't believe in a great deal of ritual—then at ten o'clock cocoa for everyone. At 10.15 bed for everyone. The dear, sweet bedroom, with the narrow white bed, by the side of which she had knelt every night so long as she could remember—even in her dear mother's day—and said her prayers.

Prayers! yes, that was a curious thing. This was the first night in her life experience when she had not said her prayers on retiring. The situation was certainly very peculiar—exceptional, one might call it.

God would understand and forgive such a lapse. And yet, after all, why—what was to prevent her saying her prayers? Of course, she couldn't kneel in the proper devotional attitude, that would be a physical impossibility; nevertheless, perhaps her prayers might be just as efficacious—if they came from the heart.

So little Miss Bracegirdle curved her body and placed her hands in a devout attitude in front of her face, and quite inaudibly murmured her prayers under the strange man's bed.

At the end she added, fervently:—

"Please God protect me from the dangers and perils of this night."

Then she lay silent and inert, strangely soothed by the effort of praying.

It began to get very uncomfortable, stuffy, but at the same time draughty, and the floor was getting harder every minute. She changed her position stealthily and controlled her desire to cough. Her heart was beating rapidly. Over and over again recurred the vivid impression of every little incident and argument that had occurred to her from the moment she left the bathroom. This must, of course, be the room next to her own. So confusing, with perhaps twenty bedrooms all exactly alike on one side of a passage—how was one to remember whether one's number was one hundred and fifteen or one hundred and sixteen? Her mind began to wander idly off into her schooldays. She was always very bad at figures. She disliked Euclid and all those subjects about angles and equations—so unimportant, not leading anywhere. History she liked, and botany, and reading about strange foreign lands, although she had always been too timid to visit them. And the lives of great people, most fascinating—Oliver Cromwell, Lord Beaconsfield, Lincoln, Grace Darling—there was a heroine for you—General Booth, a great, good man, even if a little vulgar. She remembered dear old Miss Trimmings talking about him one afternoon at the vicar of St. Bride's garden-party. She was so amusing. She—Good heavens!

Almost unwittingly Millicent Brace girdle had emitted a violent sneeze!

It was finished! For the second time that night she was conscious of her heart nearly stopping. For the second time that night she was so paralysed with fear that her mentality went to pieces. Now she would hear the man get out of bed. He would walk across to the door, switch on the light, and then lift up the frill. She could almost see that fierce moustachioed face glaring at her and growling something in French. Then he would thrust out an arm and drag her out. And then? O God in heaven! what then?

"I shall scream before he does it. Perhaps I had better scream now. If he drags me out he will clap his hand over my mouth. Perhaps chloroform—"

But somehow she could not scream. She was too frightened even for that. She lifted the frill and listened. Was he moving stealthily across the carpet? She thought—no, she couldn't be sure. Anything might be happening. He might strike her from above—with one of those heavy boots, perhaps. Nothing seemed to be happening, but the suspense was intolerable. She realized now that she hadn't the power to endure a night of it. Anything would be better than this—disgrace, imprisonment, even death. She would crawl out, wake the man, and try to explain as best she could.

She would switch on the light, cough, and say: "Monsieur!"

Then he would start up and stare at her.

Then she would say—what should she say?

"Pardon, monsieur, mais je—What on earth was the French for 'I have made a mistake'?

"J'ai tort. C'est la chambre—er—incorrect. Voulez-vous—er—?"

What was the French for "door-knob," "let me go"?

It didn't matter. She would turn on the light, cough, and trust to luck. If he got out of bed and came towards her, she would scream the hotel down.

The resolution formed, she crawled deliberately out at the foot of the bed. She scrambled hastily towards the door—a perilous journey. In a few seconds the room was flooded with light. She turned towards the bed, coughed, and cried out boldly:—

"Monsieur!"

Then for the third time that night little Miss Bracegirdle's heart all but stopped. In this case the climax of the horror took longer to develop, but when it was reached it clouded the other two experiences into insignificance.

The man on the bed was dead!

She had never beheld death before, but one does not mistake death.

She stared at him, bewildered, and repeated almost in a whisper:—

"Monsieur! Monsieur!"

Then she tip-toed towards the bed. The hair and moustache looked extraordinarily black in that grey, wax-like setting. The mouth was slightly open, and the face, which in life might have been vicious and sensual, looked incredibly peaceful and far away. It was as though she were regarding the features of a man across some vast passage of time, a being who had always been completely remote from mundane preoccupations.

When the full truth came home to her, little Miss Bracegirdle buried her face in her hands and murmured:—

"Poor fellow—poor fellow!"

For the moment her own position seemed an affair of small consequence. She was in the presence of something greater and more all-pervading. Almost instinctively she knelt by the bed and prayed.

For a few moments she seemed to be possessed by an extraordinary calmness and detachment. The burden of her hotel predicament was a gossamer trouble—a silly, trivial, almost comic episode, something that could be explained away.

But this man—he had lived his life, whatever it was like, and now he was in the presence of his Maker. What kind of man had he been?

Her meditations were broken by an abrupt sound. It was that of a pair of heavy boots being thrown down by the door outside. She started, thinking at first it was someone knocking or trying to get in. She heard the "boots," however, stumping away down the corridor, and the realization stabbed her with the truth of her own position. She mustn't stop there. The necessity to get out was even more urgent.

To be found in a strange man's bedroom in the night is bad enough, but to be found in a dead man's bedroom was even worse. They would accuse her of murder, perhaps. Yes, that would be it—how could she possibly explain to these foreigners? Good God! they would hang her. No, guillotine her—that's what they do in France. They would chop her head off with a great steel knife. Merciful heavens! She envisaged herself standing blindfold, by a priest and an executioner in a red cap, like that man in the Dickens story. What was his name?—Sydney Carton, that was it. And before he went on the scaffold he said:—

"It is a far, far better thing that I do than I have ever done—"

But no, she couldn't say that. It would be a far, far worse thing that she did. What about the dear dean; her sister-in-law arriving alone from Paraguay to-morrow; all her dear people and friends in Easingstoke; her darling Tony, the large grey tabby-cat? It was her duty not to have her head chopped off if it could possibly be avoided. She could do no good in the room. She could not recall the dead to life. Her only mission was to escape. Any minute people might arrive. The chamber-maid, the boots, the manager, the gendarmes. Visions of gendarmes arriving armed with swords and notebooks vitalized her almost exhausted energies. She was a desperate woman. Fortunately now she had not to worry about the light. She sprang once more at the door and tried to force it open with her fingers. The result hurt her and gave her pause. If she was to escape she must think, and think intensely. She mustn't do anything rash and silly; she must just think and plan calmly.

She examined the lock carefully. There was no keyhole, but there was a slip-bolt, so that the hotel guest could lock the door on the inside, but it couldn't be locked on the outside. Oh, why didn't this poor dear dead man lock his door last night? Then this trouble could not have happened. She could see the end of the steel pin. It was about half an inch down the hole. If anyone was passing they must surely notice the handle sticking out too far the other side! She drew a hairpin out of her hair and tried to coax the pin back, but she only succeeded in pushing it a little farther in. She felt the colour leaving her face, and a strange feeling of faintness came over her.

She was fighting for her life; she mustn't give way. She darted round the room like an animal in a trap, her mind alert for the slightest crevice of escape. The window had no balcony, and there was a drop of five storeys to the street below. Dawn was breaking. Soon the activities of the hotel and the city would begin. The thing must be accomplished before then.

She went back once more and stared hard at the lock. She stared at the dead man's property, his razors and brushes and writing materials. He appeared to have a lot of writing materials, pens and pencils and rubber and sealing-wax'. Sealing-wax!

Necessity is truly the mother of invention. It is in any case quite certain that Millicent Bracegirdle, who had never invented a thing in her life, would never have evolved the ingenious little device she did, had she not believed that her position was utterly desperate. For in the end this is what she did. She got together a box of matches, a candle, a bar of sealing-wax, and a hairpin. She made a little pool of hot sealing-wax, into which she dipped the end of the hairpin. Collecting a small blob on the end of it, she thrust it into the hole, and let it adhere to the end of the steel pin. At the seventh attempt she got the thing to move.

It took her just an hour and ten minutes to get that steel pin back into the room, and when at length it came far enough through for her to grip it with her fingernails, she burst into tears through the sheer physical tenseness of the strain. Very, very carefully she pulled it through, and holding it firmly with her left hand she fixed the knob with her right, then slowly turned it.

The door opened!

The temptation to dash out into the corridor and scream with relief was almost irresistible, but she forbore. She listened. She peeped out. No one was about. With beating heart she went out, closing the door inaudibly; she crept like a little mouse to the room next door, stole in, and flung herself on the bed. Immediately she did so, it flashed through her mind that she had left her sponge-bag and towel in the dead man's room!

In looking back upon her experience she always considered that that second expedition was the worst of all. She might have left the sponge-bag and towel remain there, only that the towel—she never used hotel towels—had neatly inscribed in the corner "M. B."

With furtive caution she managed to retrace her steps. She re-entered the dead man's room, reclaimed her property, and returned to her own. When the mission was accomplished she was indeed well-nigh spent. She lay on her bed and groaned feebly. At last she fell into a fevered sleep.

It was eleven o'clock when she awoke, and no one had been to disturb her. The sun was shining, and the experiences of the night appeared a dubious nightmare. Surely she had dreamt it all?

With dread still burning in her heart she rang the bell. After a short interval of time the chambermaid appeared. The girl's eyes were bright with some uncontrollable excitement. No, she had not been dreaming. This girl had heard something.

"Will you bring me some tea, please?"

"Certainly, madame."

The maid drew back the curtains and fussed about the room. She was under a pledge of secrecy, but she could contain herself no longer. Suddenly she approached the bed and whispered, excitedly:—

"Oh, madame, I am promised not to tell—but a terrible thing has happened! A man, a dead man, has been found in room one hundred and seventeen—a guest! Please not to say I tell you. But they have all been here—the gendarmes, the doctors, the inspectors. Oh, it is terrible—terrible!"

The little lady in the bed said nothing. There was indeed nothing to say. But Marie Louise Lancret was too full of emotional excitement to spare her.

"But the terrible thing is—Do you know who he was, madame? They say it is Boldhu, the man wanted for the murder of Jeanne Carreton in the barn at Vincennes. They say he strangled her, and then cut her up in pieces and hid her in two barrels, which he threw into the river. Oh, but he was a bad man, madame, a terrible bad man—and he died in the room next door. Suicide, they think; or was it an attack of the heart? Remorse; some shock, perhaps. Did you say a cafe complet, madame?"

"No, thank you, my dear—just a cup of tea—strong tea."

"Parfaitement, madame."

The girl retired, and a little later a waiter entered the room with a tray of tea. She could never get over her surprise at this. It seemed so—well, indecorous for a man—although only a waiter—to enter a lady's bedroom. There was, no doubt a great deal in what the dear dean said. They were certainly very peculiar, these French people—they had most peculiar notions. It was not the way they behaved at Easingstoke. She got farther under the sheets, but the waiter appeared quite indifferent to the situation. He put the tray down and retired.

When he had gone, she sat up and sipped her tea, which gradually wanned her. She was glad the sun was shining. She would have to get up soon. They said that her sister-in-law's boat was due to berth at one o'clock. That would give her time to dress comfortably, write to her brother, and then go down to the docks.

Poor man! So he had been a murderer, a man who cut up the bodies of his victims—and she had spent the night in his bedroom! They were certainly a most—how could she describe it?—people. Nevertheless she felt a little glad that at the end she had been there to kneel and pray by his bedside. Probably nobody else had ever done that. It was very difficult to judge people. Something at some time might have gone wrong. He might not have murdered the woman after all. People were often wrongly convicted. She herself. If the police had found her in that room at three o'clock that morning—It is that which takes place in the heart which counts. One learns and learns. Had she not learnt that one can pray just as effectively lying under a bed as kneeling beside it? Poor man!

She washed and dressed herself and walked calmly down to the writing-room. There was no evidence of excitement among the other hotel guests. Probably none of them knew about the tragedy except herself. She went to a writing-table, and after profound meditation wrote as follows:

My Dear Brother—

I arrived late last night, after a very pleasant journey. Everyone was very kind and attentive, the manager was sitting up for me. I nearly lost my spectacle case in the restaurant-car, but a kind old gentleman found them and returned them to me. There was a most amusing American child on the train. I will tell you about her on my return. The people are very pleasant, but the food is peculiar, nothing plain and wholesome. I am going down to meet Annie at one o'clock. How have you been keeping, my dear? I hope you have not had any further return of the bronchial attacks. Please tell Lizzie that I remembered in the train on the way here that that large stone jar of marmalade that Mrs. Hunt made is behind those empty tins on the top shelf of the cupboard next to the coach-house. I wonder whether Mrs. Buller was able to come to evensong after all? This is a nice hotel, but I think Annie and I will stay at the Grand to-night, as the bedrooms here are rather noisy. Well, my dear, nothing more till I return. Do take care of yourself.

Your loving sister,
Millicent.

Yes, she couldn't tell Peter about it, neither in the letter nor when she went back to him. It was her duty not to tell him. It would only distress him: she felt convinced of it. In this curious foreign atmosphere the thing appeared possible, but in Easingstoke the mere recounting of the fantastic situation would be positively indelicate. There was no escaping that broad general fact—she had spent a night in a strange man's bedroom. Whether he was a gentleman or a criminal, even whether he was dead or alive, did not seem to mitigate the jar upon her sensibilities, or, rather it would not mitigate the jar upon the peculiarly sensitive relationship between her brother and herself. To say that she had been to the bathroom, the knob of the door-handle came off in her hand, she was too frightened to awaken the sleeper or scream, she got under the bed—well, it was all perfectly true. Peter would believe her, but—one simply could not conceive such a situation in Easingstoke deanery. It would create a curious little barrier between them, as though she had been dipped in some mysterious solution which alienated her. It was her duty not to tell.

She put on her hat and went out to post the letter. She distrusted an hotel letter-box. One never knew who handled these letters. It was not a proper official way of treating them. She walked to the head post-office in Bordeaux.

The sun was shining. It was very pleasant walking about amongst these queer, excitable people, so foreign and different looking—and the cafes already crowded with chattering men and women; and the flower stalls, and the strange odour of—what was it? salt? brine? charcoal? A military band was playing in the square—very gay and moving. It was all life, and movement, and bustle—thrilling rather.

"I spent a night in a strange man's bedroom."

Little Miss Bracegirdle hunched her shoulders, hummed to herself, and walked faster. She reached the post-office, and found the large metal plate with the slot for letters and R. F. stamped above it. Something official at last! Her face was a little flushed—was it the warmth of the day, or the contact of movement and life?—as she put her letter into the slot. After posting it she put her hand into the slot and flicked it round to see that there were no foreign contraptions to impede its safe delivery. No, the letter had dropped safely in. She sighed contentedly, and walked off in the direction of the docks to meet her sister-in-law from Paraguay.

Where Was Wych Street?

In the public bar of the Wagtail, in Wapping, four men and a woman were drinking beer and discussing diseases. It was not a pretty subject, and the company was certainly not a handsome one. It was a dark November evening, and the dingy lighting of the bar seemed but to emphasize the bleak exterior. Drifts of fog and damp from without mingled with the smoke of shag. The sanded floor was kicked into a muddy morass not unlike the surface of the pavement. An old lady down the street had died from pneumonia the previous evening, and the event supplied a fruitful topic of conversation. The things that one could get! Everywhere were germs eager to destroy one. At any minute the symptoms might break out. And so, one foregathered in a cheerful spot amidst friends, and drank forgetfulness.

Prominent in this little group was Baldwin Meadows, a sallow-faced villain with battered features and prominent cheek-bones, his face cut and scarred by a hundred fights. Ex-seaman, ex-boxer, ex-fish-porter, indeed, to every one's knowledge, ex-everything. No one knew how he lived. By his side lurched an enormous coloured man who went by the name of Harry Jones. Grinning above a tankard sat a pimply-faced young man who was known as The Agent. Silver rings adorned his fingers. He had no other name, and most emphatically no address, but he "arranged things" for people, and appeared to thrive upon it in a scrambling, fugitive manner. The other two people were Mr. and Mrs. Dawes. Mr. Dawes was an entirely negative person, but Mrs. Dawes shone by virtue of a high, whining, insistent voice, keyed to within half a note of hysteria.

Then, at one point, the conversation suddenly took a peculiar turn. It came about through Mrs. Dawes mentioning that her aunt, who died from eating tinned lobster, used to work in a corset shop in Wych Street. When she said that, The Agent, whose right eye appeared to survey the ceiling, whilst his left eye looked over the other side of his tankard, remarked:

"Where was Wych Street, ma?"

"Lord!" exclaimed Mrs. Dawes. "Don't you know, dearie? You must be a young 'un, you must. Why, when I was a gal everyone knew Wych Street. It was just down there where they built the Kingsway, like."

Baldwin Meadows cleared his throat, and said:

"Wych Street used to be a turnin' runnin' from Long Acre into Wellington Street."

"Oh, no, old boy," chipped in Mr. Dawes, who always treated the ex-man with great deference. "If you'll excuse me, Wych Street was a narrow lane at the back of the old Globe Theatre, that used to pass by the church."

"I know what I'm talkin' about," growled Meadows. Mrs. Dawes's high nasal whine broke in:

"Hi, Mr. Booth, you used ter know yer wye abaht. Where was Wych Street?"

Mr. Booth, the proprietor, was polishing a tap. He looked up.

"Wych Street? Yus, of course I knoo Wych Street. Used to go there with some of the boys, when I was Covent Garden way. It was at right angles to the Strand, just east of Wellington Street."

"No, it warn't. It were alongside the Strand, before yer come to Wellington Street."

The coloured man took no part in the discussion, one street and one city being alike to him, provided he could obtain the material comforts dear to his heart; but the others carried it on with a certain amount of acerbity.

Before any agreement had been arrived at three other men entered the bar. The quick eye of Meadows recognized them at once as three of what was known at that time as "The Gallows Ring." Every member of "The Gallows Ring" had done time, but they still carried on a lucrative industry devoted to blackmail, intimidation, shoplifting, and some of the clumsier recreations. Their leader, Ben Orming, had served seven years for bashing a Chinaman down at Rotherhithe.

"The Gallows Ring" was not popular in Wapping, for the reason that many of their depredations had been inflicted upon their own class. When Meadows and Harry Jones took it into their heads to do a little wild prancing they took the trouble to go up into the West-end. They considered "The Gallows Ring" an ungentlemanly set; nevertheless, they always treated them with a certain external deference, an unpleasant crowd to quarrel with.

Ben Orming ordered beer for the three of them, and they leant against the bar and whispered in sullen accents. Something had evidently miscarried with the Ring. Mrs. Dawes continued to whine above the general drone of the bar. Suddenly she said:

"Ben, you're a hot old devil, you are. We was just 'aving a discussion like. Where was Wych Street?"

Ben scowled at her, and she continued:

"Some sez it was one place, some sez it was another. I know where it was, 'cors my aunt what died from blood p'ison, after eatin' tinned lobster, used to work at a corset shop—"

"Yus," barked Ben, emphatically. "I know where Wych Street was, it was just sarth of the river, afore yer come to Waterloo Station."

It was then that the coloured man, who up to that point had taken no part in the discussion, thought fit to intervene.

"Nope. You's all wrong, cap'n. Wych Street were alongside de church, way over where the Strand takes a side-line up west."

Ben turned on him fiercely.

"What the blazes does a blanketty nigger know abaht it? I've told yer where Wych Street was."

"Yus, and I know where it was," interposed Meadows.

"Yer both wrong. Wych Street was a turning running from Long Acre into Wellington Street."

"I didn't ask yer what you thought," growled Ben.

"Well, I suppose I've a right to an opinion?"

"You always think you know everything, you do."

"You can just keep yer mouth shut."

"It 'ud take more'n you to shut it."

Mr. Booth thought it advisable at this juncture to bawl across the bar:

"Now, gentlemen, no quarrelling, please."

The affair might have been subsided at that point, but for Mrs. Dawes. Her emotions over the death of the old lady in the street had been so stirred that she had been, almost unconsciously, drinking too much gin. She suddenly screamed out:

"Don't you take no lip from 'im, Mr. Medders. The dirty, thieving devil, 'e always thinks 'e's goin' to come it over every one."

She stood up threateningly, and one of Ben's supporters gave her a gentle push backwards. In three minutes the bar was in a complete state of pandemonium. The three members of "The Gallows Ring" fought two men and a woman, for Mr. Dawes merely stood in a corner and screamed out:

"Don't! Don't!"

Mrs. Dawes stabbed the man who had pushed her through the wrist with a hatpin. Meadows and Ben Orming closed on each other and fought savagely with the naked fists. A lucky blow early in the encounter sent Meadows reeling against the wall, with blood streaming down his temple. Then the coloured man hurled a pewter tankard straight at Ben and it hit him on the knuckles. The pain maddened him to a frenzy. His other supporter had immediately got to grips with Harry Jones, and picked up one of the high stools and, seizing an opportunity, brought it down crash on to the coloured man's skull.

The whole affair was a matter of minutes. Mr. Booth was bawling out in the street. A whistle sounded. People were running in all directions.

"Beat it! Beat it for God's sake!" called the man who had been stabbed through the wrist. His face was very white, and he was obviously about to faint.

Ben and the other man, whose name was Toller, dashed to the door. On the pavement there was a confused scramble. Blows were struck indiscriminately. Two policemen appeared. One was laid hors de combat by a kick on the knee-cap from Toller. The two men fled into the darkness, followed by a hue-and-cry. Born and bred in the locality, they took every advantage of their knowledge. They tacked through alleys and raced down dark mews, and clambered over walls. Fortunately for them, the people they passed, who might have tripped them up or aided in the pursuit, merely fled indoors. The people in Wapping are not always on the side of the pursuer. But the police held on. At last Ben and Toller slipped through the door of an empty house in Aztec Street barely ten yards ahead of their nearest pursuer. Blows rained on the door, but they slipped the bolts, and then fell panting to the floor. When Ben could speak, he said:

"If they cop us, it means swinging."

"Was the nigger done in?"

"I think so. But even if 'e wasn't, there was that other affair the night before last. The game's up."

The ground-floor rooms were shuttered and bolted, but they knew that the police would probably force the front door. At the back there was no escape, only a narrow stable yard, where lanterns were already flashing. The roof only extended thirty yards either way and the police would probably take possession of it. They made a round of the house, which was sketchily furnished. There was a loaf, a small piece of mutton, and a bottle of pickles, and, the most precious possession, three bottles of whisky. Each man drank half a glass of neat whisky; then Ben said: "We'll be able to keep 'em quiet for a bit, anyway," and he went and fetched an old twelve-bore gun and a case of cartridges. Toller was opposed to this last desperate resort, but Ben continued to murmur, "It means swinging, anyway."

And thus began the notorious siege of Aztec Street. It lasted three days and four nights. You may remember that, on forcing a panel of the front door, Sub-Inspector Wraithe, of the V Division, was shot through the chest. The police then tried other methods. A hose was brought into play without effect. Two policemen were killed and four wounded. The military was requisitioned. The street was picketed. Snipers occupied windows of the houses opposite. A distinguished member of the Cabinet drove down in a motor-car, and directed operations in a top-hat. It was the introduction of poison-gas which was the ultimate cause of the downfall of the citadel. The body of Ben Orming was never found, but that of Toller was discovered near the front door with a bullet through his heart. The medical officer to the Court pronounced that the man had been dead three days, but whether killed by a chance bullet from a sniper or whether killed deliberately by his fellow-criminal was never revealed. For when the end came Orming had apparently planned a final act of venom. It was known that in the basement a considerable quantity of petrol had been stored. The contents had probably been carefully distributed over the most inflammable materials in the top rooms. The fire broke out, as one witness described it, "almost like an explosion." Orming must have perished in this. The roof blazed up, and the sparks carried across the yard and started a stack of light timber in the annexe of Messrs. Morrel's piano-factory. The factory and two blocks of tenement buildings were burnt to the ground. The estimated cost of the destruction was one hundred and eighty thousand pounds. The casualties amounted to seven killed and fifteen wounded.

At the inquiry held under Chief Justice Pengammon various odd interesting facts were revealed. Mr. Lowes-Parlby, the brilliant young K.C., distinguished himself by his searching cross-examination of many witnesses. At one point a certain Mrs. Dawes was put in the box.

"Now," said Mr. Lowes-Parlby, "I understand that on the evening in question, Mrs. Dawes, you, and the victims, and these other people who have been mentioned, were all seated in the public bar of the Wagtail, enjoying its no doubt excellent hospitality and indulging in a friendly discussion. Is that so?"

"Yes, sir."

"Now, will you tell his lordship what you were discussing?"

"Diseases, sir."

"Diseases! And did the argument become acrimonious?"

"Pardon?"

"Was there a serious dispute about diseases?"

"No, sir."

"Well, what was the subject of the dispute?"

"We was arguin' as to where Wych Street was, sir."

"What's that?" said his lordship.

"The witness states, my lord, that they were arguing as to where Wych Street was."

"Wych Street? Do you mean W-Y-C-H?"

"Yes, sir."

"You mean the narrow old street that used to run across the site of what is now the Gaiety Theatre?"

Mr. Lowes-Parlby smiled in his most charming manner.

"Yes, my lord, I believe the witness refers to the same street you mention, though, if I may be allowed to qualify your lordship's description of the locality, may I suggest that it was a little further east, at the side of the old Globe Theatre, which was adjacent to St. Martin's in the Strand? That is the street you were all arguing about, isn't it, Mrs. Dawes?"

"Well, sir, my aunt who died from eating tinned lobster used to work at a corset-shop. I ought to know."

His lordship ignored the witness. He turned to the counsel rather peevishly.

"Mr. Lowes-Parlby, when I was your age I used to pass through Wych Street every day of my life. I did so for nearly twelve years. I think it hardly necessary for you to contradict me."

The counsel bowed. It was not his place to dispute with a chief justice, although that chief justice be a hopeless old fool; but another eminent K.C., an elderly man with a tawny beard, rose in the body of the court, and said:

"If I may be allowed to interpose, your lordship, I also spent a great deal of my youth passing through Wych Street. I have gone into the matter, comparing past and present ordnance survey maps. If I am not mistaken, the street the witness was referring to began near the hoarding at the entrance to Kingsway and ended at the back of what is now the Aldwych Theatre."

"Oh, no, Mr. Backer!" exclaimed Lowes-Parlby.

His lordship removed his glasses and snapped out:

"The matter is entirely irrelevant to the case."

It certainly was, but the brief passage-of-arms left an unpleasant tang of bitterness behind. It was observed that Mr. Lowes-Parlby never again quite got the prehensile grip upon his cross-examination that he had shown in his treatment of the earlier witnesses. The coloured man, Harry Jones, had died in hospital, but Mr. Booth, the proprietor of the Wagtail, Baldwin Meadows, Mr. Dawes, and the man who was stabbed in the wrist, all gave evidence of a rather nugatory character. Lowes-Parlby could do nothing with it. The findings of this Special Inquiry do not concern us. It is sufficient to say that the witnesses already mentioned all returned to Wapping. The man who had received the thrust of a hatpin through his wrist did not think it advisable to take any action against Mrs. Dawes. He was pleasantly relieved to find that he was only required as a witness of an abortive discussion.

In a few weeks' time the great Aztec Street siege remained only a romantic memory to the majority of Londoners. To Lowes-Parlby the little dispute with Chief Justice Pengammon rankled unreasonably. It is annoying to be publicly snubbed for making a statement which you know to be absolutely true, and which you have even taken pains to verify. And Lowes-Parlby was a young man accustomed to score. He made a point of looking everything up, of being prepared for an adversary thoroughly. He liked to give the appearance of knowing everything. The brilliant career just ahead of him at times dazzled him. He was one of the darlings of the gods. Everything came to Lowes-Parlby. His father had distinguished himself at the bar before him, and had amassed a modest fortune. He was an only son. At Oxford he had carried off every possible degree. He was already being spoken of for very high political honours. But the most sparkling jewel in the crown of his successes was Lady Adela Charters, the daughter of Lord Vermeer, the Minister for Foreign Affairs. She was his fiancée, and it was considered the most brilliant match of the season. She was young and almost pretty, and Lord Vermeer was immensely wealthy and one of the most influential men in Great Britain. Such a combination was irresistible. There seemed to be nothing missing in the life of Francis Lowes-Parlby, K.C.

One of the most regular and absorbed spectators at the Aztec Street inquiry was old Stephen Garrit. Stephen Garrit held a unique but quite inconspicuous position in the legal world at that time. He was a friend of judges, a specialist at various abstruse legal rulings, a man of remarkable memory, and yet, an amateur. He had never taken sick, never eaten the requisite dinners, never passed an examination in his life; but the law of evidence was meat and drink to him. He passed his life in the Temple, where he had chambers. Some of the most eminent counsel in the world would take his opinion, or come to him for advice. He was very old, very silent, and very absorbed. He attended every meeting of the Aztec Street inquiry, but from beginning to end he never volunteered an opinion.

After the inquiry was over he went and visited an old friend at the London Survey Office. He spent two mornings examining maps. After that he spent two mornings pottering about the Strand, Kingsway, and Aldwych; then he worked out some careful calculations on a ruled chart. He entered the particulars in a little book which he kept for purposes of that kind, and then retired to his chambers to study other matters. But before doing so, he entered a little apophthegm in another book. It was apparently a book in which he intended to compile a summary of his legal experiences. The sentence ran:

"The basic trouble is that people make statements without sufficient data."

Old Stephen need not have appeared in this story at all, except for the fact that he was present at the dinner at Lord Vermeer's, where a rather deplorable incident occurred. And you must acknowledge that in the circumstances it is useful to have such a valuable and efficient witness.

Lord Vermeer was a competent, forceful man, a little quick-tempered and autocratic. He came from Lancashire, and before entering politics had made an enormous fortune out of borax, artificial manure, and starch.

It was a small dinner-party, with a motive behind it. His principal guest was Mr. Sandeman, the London agent of the Ameer of Bakkan. Lord Vermeer was very anxious to impress Mr. Sandeman and to be very friendly with him: the reasons will appear later. Mr. Sandeman was a self-confessed cosmopolitan. He spoke seven languages and professed to be equally at home in any capital in Europe. London had been his headquarters for over twenty years. Lord Vermeer also invited Mr. Arthur Toombs, a colleague in the Cabinet, his prospective son-in-law, Lowes-Parlby, K.C., James Trolley, a very tame Socialist M.P., and Sir Henry and Lady Breyd, the two latter being invited, not because Sir Henry was of any use, but because Lady Breyd was a pretty and brilliant woman who might amuse his principal guest. The sixth guest was Stephen Garrit.

The dinner was a great success. When the succession of courses eventually came to a stop, and the ladies had retired, Lord Vermeer conducted his male guests into another room for a ten minutes' smoke before re-joining them. It was then that the unfortunate incident occurred. There was no love lost between Lowes-Parlby and Mr. Sandeman. It is difficult to ascribe the real reason of their mutual animosity, but on the several occasions when they had met there had invariably passed a certain sardonic by-play. They were both clever, both comparatively young, each a little suspect and jealous of the other; moreover, it was said in some quarters that Mr. Sandeman had had intentions himself with regard to Lord Vermeer's daughter, that he had been on the point of a proposal when Lowes-Parlby had butted in and forestalled him. Mr. Sandeman had dined well, and he was in the mood to dazzle with a display of his varied knowledge and experiences. The conversation drifted from a discussion of the rival claims of great cities to the slow, inevitable removal of old landmarks. There had been a slightly acrimonious disagreement between Lowes-Parlby and Mr. Sandeman as to the claims of Budapest and Lisbon, and Mr. Sandeman had scored because he extracted from his rival a confession that, though he had spent two months in Budapest, he had only spent two days in Lisbon. Mr. Sandeman had lived for four years in either city. Lowes-Parlby changed the subject abruptly.

"Talking of landmarks," he said, "we had a queer point arise in that Aztec Street inquiry. The original dispute arose owing to a discussion between a crowd of people in a pub as to where Wych Street was."

"I remember," said Lord Vermeer. "A perfectly absurd discussion. Why, I should have thought that any man over forty would remember exactly where it was."

"Where would you say it was, sir?" asked Lowes-Parlby.

"Why to be sure, it ran from the corner of Chancery Lane and ended at the second turning after the Law Courts, going west."

Lowes-Parlby was about to reply, when Mr. Sandeman cleared his throat and said, in his supercilious, oily voice:

"Excuse me, my lord. I know my Paris, and Vienna, and Lisbon, every brick and stone, but I look upon London as my home. I know my London even better. I have a perfectly clear recollection of Wych Street. When I was a student I used to visit there to buy books. It ran parallel to New Oxford Street on the south side, just between it and Lincoln's Inn Fields."

There was something about this assertion that infuriated Lowes-Parlby. In the first place, it was so hopelessly wrong and so insufferably asserted. In the second place, he was already smarting under the indignity of being shown up about Lisbon. And then there suddenly flashed through his mind the wretched incident when he had been publicly snubbed by Justice Pengammon about the very same point; and he knew that he was right each time. Damn Wych Street! He turned on Mr. Sandeman.

"Oh, nonsense! You may know something about these, eastern cities; you certainly know nothing about London if you make a statement like that. Wych Street was a little further east of what is now the Gaiety Theatre. It used to run by the side of the old Globe Theatre, parallel to the Strand."

The dark moustache of Mr. Sandeman shot upwards, revealing a narrow line of yellow teeth. He uttered a sound that was a mingling of contempt and derision; then he drawled out:

"Really? How wonderful, to have such comprehensive knowledge!"

He laughed, and his small eyes fixed his rival. Lowes-Parlby flushed a deep red. He gulped down half a glass of port and muttered just above a whisper: "Damned impudence!" Then, in the rudest manner he could display, he turned his back deliberately on Sandeman and walked out of the room.

In the company of Adela he tried to forget the little contretemps. The whole thing was so absurd, so utterly undignified. As though he didn't know! It was the little accumulation of pin-pricks all arising out of that one argument. The result had suddenly goaded him to, well, being rude, to say the least of it. It wasn't that Sandeman mattered. To the devil with Sandeman! But what would his future father-in-law think? He had never before given way to any show of ill-temper before him. He forced himself into a mood of rather fatuous jocularity. Adela was at her best in those moods. They would have lots of fun together in the days to come. Her almost pretty, not too clever face was dimpled with kittenish glee. Life was a tremendous rag to her. They were expecting Toccata, the famous opera-singer. She had been engaged at a very high fee to come on from Covent Garden. Mr. Sandeman was very fond of music. Adela was laughing, and discussing which was the most honourable position for the great Sandeman to occupy. There came to Lowes-Parlby a sudden abrupt misgiving. What sort of wife would this be to him when they were not just fooling? He immediately dismissed the curious, furtive little stab of doubt. The splendid proportions of the room calmed his senses. A huge bowl of dark red roses quickened his perceptions. His career.... The door opened. But it was not La Toccata. It was one of the household flunkies. Lowes-Parlby turned again to his inamorata.

"Excuse me, sir. His lordship says will you kindly go and see him in the library?"

Lowes-Parlby regarded the messenger, and his heart beat quickly. An uncontrollable presage of evil racked his nerve-centres. Something had gone wrong; and yet the whole thing was so absurd, trivial. In a crisis, well, he could always apologize. He smiled confidently at Adela, and said:

"Why, of course; with pleasure. Please excuse me, dear." He followed the impressive servant out of the room. His foot had barely touched the carpet of the library when he realized that his worst apprehensions were to be plumbed to the depths. For a moment he thought Lord Vermeer was alone, then he observed old Stephen Garrit, lying in an easy-chair in the corner like a piece of crumpled parchment. Lord Vermeer did not beat about the bush. When the door was closed, he bawled out, savagely:

"What the devil have you done?"

"Excuse me, sir. I'm afraid I don't understand. Is it Sandeman?"

"Sandeman has gone."

"Oh, I'm sorry."

"Sorry! By God, I should think you might be sorry! You insulted him. My prospective son-in-law insulted him in my own house!"

"I'm awfully sorry. I didn't realize."

"Realize! Sit down, and don't assume for one moment that you continue to be my prospective son-in-law. Your insult was a most intolerable piece of effrontery, not only to him, but to me."

"But I—"

"Listen to me. Do you know that the government were on the verge of concluding a most far-reaching treaty with that man? Do you know that the position was just touch-and-go? The concessions we were prepared to make would have cost the State thirty million pounds, and it would have been cheap. Do you hear that? It would have been cheap! Bakkan is one of the most vulnerable outposts of the Empire. It is a terrible danger-zone. If certain powers can usurp our authority, and, mark you, the whole blamed place is already riddled with this new pernicious doctrine, you know what I mean, before we know where we are the whole East will be in a blaze.

India! My God! This contract we were negotiating would have countered this outward thrust. And you, you blockhead, you come here and insult the man upon whose word the whole thing depends."

"I really can't see, sir, how I should know all this."

"You can't see it! But, you fool, you seemed to go out of your way. You insulted him about the merest quibble, in my house!"

"He said he knew where Wych Street was. He was quite wrong. I corrected him."

"Wych Street! Wych Street be damned! If he said Wych Street was in the moon, you should have agreed with him. There was no call to act in the way you did. And you, you think of going into politics!"

The somewhat cynical inference of this remark went unnoticed. Lowes-Parlby was too unnerved. He mumbled:

"I'm very sorry."

"I don't want your sorrow. I want something more practical."

"What's that, sir?"

"You will drive straight to Mr. Sandeman's, find him, and apologize. Tell him you find that he was right about Wych Street after all. If you can't find him to-night, you must find him to-morrow morning. I give you till midday to-morrow. If by that time you have not offered a handsome apology to Mr. Sandeman, you do not enter this house again, you do not see my daughter again. Moreover, all the power I possess will be devoted to hounding you out of that profession you have dishonoured. Now you can go."

Dazed and shaken, Lowes-Parlby drove back to his flat at Knightsbridge. Before acting he must have time to think. Lord Vermeer had given him till to-morrow midday. Any apologizing that was done should be done after a night's reflection. The fundamental purposes of his being were to be tested. He knew that. He was at a great crossing. Some deep instinct within him was grossly outraged. Is it that a point comes when success demands that a man shall sell his soul? It was all so absurdly trivial, a mere argument about the position of a street that had ceased to exist. As Lord Vermeer said, what did it matter about Wych Street?

Of course he should apologize. It would hurt horribly to do so, but would a man sacrifice everything on account of some footling argument about a street?

In his own rooms, Lowes-Parlby put on a dressing-gown, and, lighting a pipe, he sat before the fire. He would have given anything for companionship at such a moment, the right companionship. How lovely it would be to have, a woman, just the right woman, to talk this all over with; someone who understood and sympathized. A sudden vision came to him of Adela's face grinning about the prospective visit of La Toccata, and again the low voice of misgiving whispered in his ears. Would Adela be, just the right woman? In very truth, did he really love Adela? Or was it all, a rag? Was life a rag, a game played by lawyers, politicians, and people?

The fire burned low, but still he continued to sit thinking, his mind principally occupied with the dazzling visions of the future. It was past midnight when he suddenly muttered a low "Damn!" and walked to the bureau. He took up a pen and wrote:

"Dear Mr. Sandeman, I must apologize for acting so rudely to you last night. It was quite unpardonable of me, especially as I since find, on going into the matter, that you were quite right about the position of Wych Street. I can't think how I made the mistake. Please forgive me.

"Yours cordially,

"FRANCIS LOWES-PARLBY."

Having written this, he sighed and went to bed. One might have imagined at that point that the matter was finished. But there are certain little greedy demons of conscience that require a lot of stilling, and they kept Lowes-Parlby awake more than half the night. He kept on repeating to himself, "It's all positively absurd!" But the little greedy demons pranced around the bed, and they began to group things into two definite issues. On the one side, the great appearances; on the other, something at the back of it all, something deep, fundamental, something that could only be expressed by one word, truth. If he had really loved Adela, if he weren't so absolutely certain that Sandeman was wrong and he was right, why should he have to say that Wych Street was where it wasn't? "Isn't there, after all," said one of the little demons, "something which makes for greater happiness than success? Confess this, and we'll let you sleep."

Perhaps that is one of the most potent weapons the little demons possess. However full our lives may be, we ever long for moments of tranquillity. And conscience holds before our eyes some mirror of an ultimate tranquillity. Lowes-Parlby was certainly not himself. The gay, debonair, and brilliant egoist was tortured, and tortured almost beyond control; and it had all apparently risen through the ridiculous discussion about a street. At a quarter past three in the morning he arose from his bed with a groan, and, going into the other room, he tore the letter to Mr. Sandeman to pieces.

Three weeks later old Stephen Garrit was lunching with the Lord Chief Justice. They were old friends, and they never found it incumbent to be very conversational. The lunch was an excellent, but frugal, meal. They both ate slowly and thoughtfully, and their drink was water. It was not till they reached the dessert stage that his lordship indulged in any very informative comment, and then he recounted to Stephen the details of a recent case in which he considered that the presiding judge had, by an unprecedented paralogy, misinterpreted the law of evidence. Stephen listened with absorbed attention. He took two cob-nuts from the silver dish, and turned them over meditatively, without cracking them. When his lordship had completely stated his opinion and peeled a pear, Stephen mumbled:

"I have been impressed, very impressed indeed. Even in my own field of limited observation, the opinion of an outsider, you may say, so often it happens, the trouble caused by an affirmation without sufficiently established data. I have seen lives lost, ruin brought about, endless suffering. Only last week, a young man, a brilliant career, almost shattered. People make statements without"

He put the nuts back on the dish, and then, in an apparently irrelevant manner, he said abruptly:

"Do you remember Wych Street, my lord?"

The Lord Chief justice grunted.

"Wych Street! Of course I do."

"Where would you say it was, my lord?"

"Why, here, of course."

His lordship took a pencil from his pocket and sketched a plan on the tablecloth.

"It used to run from there to here."

Stephen adjusted his glasses and carefully examined the plan. He took a long time to do this, and when he had finished his hand instinctively went towards a breast pocket where he kept a note-book with little squared pages. Then he stopped and sighed. After all, why argue with the law? The law was like that, an excellent thing, not infallible, of course (even the plan of the Lord Chief Justice was a quarter of a mile out), but still an excellent, a wonderful thing. He examined the bony knuckles of his hands and yawned slightly.

"Do you remember it?" said the Lord Chief Justice.

Stephen nodded sagely, and his voice seemed to come from a long way off:

"Yes, I remember it, my lord. It was a melancholy little street."

The Octave of Jealousy

I

A tramp came through a cutting by old Jerry Shindle's nursery, and crossing the stile, stepped into the glare of the white road. He was a tall swarthy man with stubbly red whiskers which appeared to conceal the whole of his face, except a small portion under each eye about the size of a two shilling piece. His skin showed through the rents in a filthy old black green garment, and was the same colour as his face, a livid bronze. His toes protruded from his boots, which seemed to be home-made contraptions of canvas and string. He carried an ash stick, and the rest of his worldly belongings in a spotted red and white handkerchief. His worldly belongings consisted of some rags, a door-knob, a portion of a foot-rule, a tin mug stolen from a workhouse, half a dozen date stones, a small piece of very old bread, a raw onion, the shutter of a camera, and two empty matchboxes.

He looked up and down the road as though uncertain of his direction. To the north it curved under the wooded opulence of Crawshay Park. To the south it stretched like a white ribbon across a bold vista of shadeless downs. He was hungry and he eyed, critically, the potential possibilities of a cottage standing back from the road. It was a shabby little three-roomed affair with fowls running in and out of the front door, some washing on a line, and the sound of a child crying within. While he was hesitating, a farm labourer came through a gate to an adjoining field, and walked towards the cottage. He, too, carried property tied up in a red handkerchief. His other hand balanced a steel fork across his left shoulder. He was a thick-set, rather dour-looking man. As he came up the tramp said:

"Where does this road lead to, mate?" The labourer replied brusquely: "Pondhurst."

"How far?"

"Three and a half miles." Without embroidering this information any further he walked stolidly across the road and entered the garden of the cottage. The tramp watched him put the fork down by the lintel of the door: He saw him enter the cottage, and he heard a woman's voice. He sighed and muttered into his stubbly red beard:

"Lucky devil!" Then, hunching his shoulders, he set out with long flat-footed strides down the white road which led across the downs.

II

Having kicked some mud off his boots, the labourer, Martin Crosby, said to his wife:

"Dinner ready?" Emma Crosby was wringing out some clothes. Her face was shiny with the steam and the heat of the day.

She answered petulantly:

"No, it isn't. You'll have to wait another ten minutes, the 'taters aren't cooked. I've enough to do this morning I can tell yer, what with the washing, and Lizzie screaming with her teeth, and the boiler going wrong."

"Ugh! There's alius somethin'." Martin knew there was no appeal against delay. He had been married four years; he knew his wife's temper and mode of life sufficiently well. He went out into the garden and lighted his pipe. The fowls clucked round his feet and he kicked them away. He, too, was hungry.

However, there would be food of a sort-in time. Some greasy pudding and potatoes boiled to a liquid mash, a piece of cheese perhaps. Well, there it was. When you work in the open air all day you can eat anything. The sun was pleasant on his face, the shag pungent and comforting. If only old Emma weren't such a muddler! A good enough piece of goods when at her best, but always in a muddle, always behind time, no management, and then resentful because things went wrong.

Lizzie: seven months old and two teeth through already and another coming. A lovely child, the spit and image of-what her mother must have been. Next time it would be a boy. Life wasn't so bad-really.

The gate clicked, and the tall figure of Ambrose Baines appeared. He was dressed in a corduroy coat and knickers, stout brown gaiters and square thick boots.

Tucked under his arm was a gun with its two barrels pointing at the ground. He was the gamekeeper to Sir Septimus Letter. He stood just inside the gate and called out:

"Momin', Martin." Martin replied: "Momin'."

"I was just passin'. The missus says you can have a cookin' or so of runner beans if you wants 'em. We've got more than enough, and I hear as yours is blighty."

"Oh! ay, thank'ee." "Middlin' hot to-day."

"Ay terrible hot."

"When'll you be comin'?"

"I'll stroll over now. There's nowt to do. I'm waitin' dinner. I 'specks it'll be a half-hour or so. You know what Emm is." He went inside and fetched a basket. He said nothing to his wife, but rejoined Baines in the road.

They strolled through the cutting and got into the back of the gamekeeper's garden just inside the wood.

Martin went along the row and filled his basket. Baines left him and went into his cottage. He could hear Mrs. Baines singing and washing up.

Of course they had had their dinner. It would be like that. Mrs. Baines was a marvel. On one or two occasions Martin had entered their cottage. Everything was spick and span, and done on time. The two children always seemed to be clean and quiet. There were pretty pink curtains and framed oleographs. Mrs.

Baines could cook, and she led the hymns at church- so they said. Even the garden was neat, and trim, and fruitful. Of course their runner beans would be prolific whilst his failed. Mrs. Baines appeared at the door and called out:

"Momin', Mr. Crosby." He replied gruffly: "Mornin', Mrs. Baines." "Middlin' hot."

"Ay ... terrible hot." She was not what you would call a pretty, attractive woman; but she was natty, competent, irrepressibly cheerful. She would make a shilling go as far as Emma would a pound. The cottage had five rooms, all in a good state of repair. The roof had been newly thatched.

All this was done for him, of course, by his employer.

He paid no rent; Martin had to pay five shillings a week, and then the roof leaked, and the boiler never worked properly-but perhaps that was Emm's fault.

He picked up his basket and strolled towards the outer gate. As he did so, he heard the two children laughing, and Baines' voice joining in.

"Some people do have luck," Martin murmured, and went back to his wife.

III

"Jack and Jill went up the hill
To fetch a pail of water;
Jack fell down and broke his crown
And Jill came tumbling after!"

It was very pretty-the way Winny Baines sang that, balancing the smaller boy on her knee, and jerking him skywards on the last word. Not what the world would call a pretty woman, but pretty enough to Ambrose, with her clear skin, kind motherly eyes, and thin brown hair. Her voice had a quality which somehow always expressed her gentle and unconquerable nature.

"She's too good for me," Ambrose would think at odd moments. "She didn't ought to be a gamekeeper's wife. She ought to be a lady-with carriages, and comforts, and well-dressed friends." The reflection would stir in him a feeling of sullen resentment, tempered with pride. She was a wonderful woman. She managed so well; she never complained.

Of course, so far as the material necessities were concerned, there was enough and to spare. The cottage was comfortable, and reasonably well furnished so far as he could determine. Of food there was abundance; game, rabbits, vegetables, eggs, fruit. The only thing he had to buy in the way of food was milk from the farm, and a few groceries from Mr. Meads' shop. He paid nothing for the cottage, and yet-he would have liked to have made things better for Winny.

His wages were small, and there were clothes to buy, all kinds of little incidental expenses. There never seemed a chance to save and soon there would be the boy's schooling.

In spite of the small income, Winny always managed to keep herself and the children neat and smart, and even to help others like the more unfortunate Crosbys.

She did all the work of the cottage, the care of the children, the mending and washing, and still found time to make jam, to preserve fruit, to grow flowers, and to sing in the church choir. She was the daughter of a piano tuner at Bladestone, and the glamour of this early connection always hung between Ambrose and herself.

To him a piano-tuner appeared a remote and romantic figure. It suggested a world of concerts, theatres, and Bohemian life. He was never quite clear about the precise functions of a piano-tuner, but he regarded his wife as the daughter of a public man, coming from a world far removed from the narrow limits of the life she was forced to lead with him.

In spite of her repeated professions of happiness, Ambrose always felt a shade suspicious, not of her, but of his own ability to satisfy her every demand.

Sometimes he would observe her looking round the little rooms, as though she were visualizing what they might contain. Perhaps she wanted a grand piano, or some inlaid chairs, or embroidered coverings. He had not the money to buy these things, and he knew that she would never ask for them; but still it was there-that queer gnawing sense of insecurity. At dawn he would wander through the coppices, drenched in dew, the gun under his arm, and the dog close to heel. The sunlight would come rippling over the jewelled leaves, and little clumps of primroses and violets would reveal themselves.

Life would be good then, and yet somehow-it was not Winnie's life. Only through their children did they seem to know each other.

"Jack and Jill went up the hill
To fetch a pail of water;
Jack fell down and broke His crown
And Jill came tumbling after!"

"Oo—Ambrose," the other boy was tugging at his beard, when Winny spoke. He pretended to scream with pain before he turned to his wife.

"Yes, my dear?"

"Will you be passing Mr. Meads' shop? We have run out of candles."

"Oh? Roight be, my love. I'll be nigh there afore sundown. I have to order seed from Crumblings." He was later than he expected at Mr. Meads' shop.

He had to wait whilst several women were being served.

The portly owner's new cash register went "tap-tapping!" five times before he got a chance to say:

"Evenin', Mr. Meads, give us a pound of candles, will ye?" Mrs. Meads came in through a parlour

at the back, in a rustling black dress. She was going to a welfare meeting at the vicar's. She said:

"Good evening, Mr. Baines, hope you are all nicely." A slightly disturbing sight met the eye of Ambrose.

The parlour door was open, and he could see a maid in a cap and apron clearing away tea things in the gaily furnished room. The Meads had got a servant! He knew that Meads was extending his business. He had a cheap clothing department now, and he was building a shed out at the back with the intention of supplying petrol to casual motorists, but-a servant! He picked up his packet of candles and muttered gruffly:

"Good evenin'." Before he had reached the door he heard" Tap-tapping!" His one and twopence had gone into the box.

As he swung down the village street, he muttered to himself:

"God! I wish I had his money!"

IV

When Mrs. Meads returned from the Welfare meeting at half-past eight, she found Mr. Meads waiting for her in the parlour, and the supper laid. There was cold veal and beetroot, apple pie, cheese and stout.

"I'm sorry I'm late, dear," she said.

"That's all right, my love," replied Mr. Meads, not looking up from his newspaper.

"We had a lovely meeting-Mrs. Wonnicott was there, and Mrs. Beal, and Mrs. Edwin Pillcreak, and Mrs. James, and Ada, and both the Jamiesons, and the Vicar was perfectly sweet. He made two lovely speeches."

"Oh, that was nice," said Mr. Meads, trying to listen and read a piquant paragraph about a divorce case at the same time.

"I should think you want your supper."

"I'm ready when you are, my love." Mr. Meads put down his newspaper, and drawing his chair up to the table, began to set about the veal. He was distinctly a man for his victuals. He carved rapidly for

her, and less rapidly for himself. From this you must not imagine that he treated his wife meanly. On the contrary, he gave her a large helping, but a close observer could not help detecting that when carving for himself he seemed to take more interest in his job. Then he rang a little tinkly hand-bell and the new maid appeared.

"Go into the shop, my dear," he said," and get me a pot of pickled walnuts from the second shelf on the left before you come to them bales of calico." The maid went, and Mrs. Meads clucked:

"Um-being a bit extravagant to-night, John." "The labourer is worthy of his hire," quoted Mr. Meads sententiously. He put up a barrage of veal in the forefront of his mouth-he had no back teeth, but managed to penetrate it with an opaque rumble of sound. "Besides we had a good day to-day—done a lot of business. Pass the stout"

"I'm glad to hear it," replied Mrs. Meads. "It's about time things began to improve, considerin' what we've been through. Mrs. Wonnicott was wearin' her biscuit-coloured taffeta with a new lace yoke. She looked smart, but a bit stiff for the Welfare to my way of thinkin'."

"Ah!" came rumbling through the veal.

"Oh, and did I tell you Mrs. Mounthead was there, too? She was wearing her starched ninon—no end of a swell she looked." Mr. Mead's eyes lighted with a definite interest at last. Mrs. Mounthead was the wife of James Mounthead, the proprietor of that handsome hostelry, "The Die is Cast." When his long day's work was over Mr. Meads would not infrequently pop into "The Die is Cast" for an hour or so before closing time and have a long chat with Mr. James Mounthead. He swallowed half a glass of stout at a gulp, and helped himself liberally to the pickled walnuts which the maid had just brought in. Eyeing the walnuts thoughtfully he said:

"Oh, so she's got into it, too, has she?"

"Yes, she's really quite a pleasant body. She told me coming down the street that her husband has just bought Balder's farm over at Pondhurst. He's setting up his son there who's marrying Kate Steyning. Her people have got a bit of money, too, so they'll be all right. By the way we haven't heard from Charlie for nearly three weeks." Mr. Meads sighed. Why were women always like that? There was Edie. He was trying to tell her that things were improving, going well in fact. The shed for petrol and motor accessories was nearly finished; the cheap clothing department was in full swing; he had indulged in pickled walnuts for supper (her supper, too); and there she must needs talk about-Charlie! Everybody in the neighbourhood knew that their son Charlie was up in London, and not doing himself or anybody else any good. And almost in the same breath she must needs talk about old Mounthead's son. Everyone knew that young Mounthead was a promising, industrious fellow. Oh! and so James had bought him Balder's farm, had he? That cost a pretty penny, he knew. Just bought a farm, had he? Not put the money into his business; just bought it in the way that he, Sam Meads, might buy a gramophone, or an umbrella. Psaugh!

"I don't want no tart," he said, on observing Edie begin to carve it.

"No tart!" she exclaimed. "Why, what's wrong?"

"Oh, I don't know," he replied. "Don't feel like it-working too hard-bit flatulent. I'll go out for a stroll after supper." An hour later he was leaning against the bar of "The Die is Cast," drinking gin and water, and listening to Mr. Mounthead discourse on dogs. The bar of "The Die is Cast" was a self-constituted village club. Other cronies drifted in. They were all friends of both Mr. Meads and Mr. Mounthead. Mrs. Mounthead seldom appeared in the bar, but there was a potman and a barmaid named Florrie; and somewhere in the rear a cook, two housemaids, a scullery maid, a boy for knives and boots, and an ostler. Mr. Mounthead had a victoria and a governess car, as well as a van for business purposes, a brown mare and a pony. He also had his own farm, well stocked with pigs, cattle, and poultry.

While taking his guests' money in a sleepy leisurely way, he regaled them with the rich fruits of his opinions and experiences. Later on he dropped casually that he was engaging an overseer at four hundred a year to take his son's place. And Mr. Meads glanced round the bar and noted the shining glass and pewter, the polished mahogany, the little pink and green glasses winking at him insolently.

"He doesn't know what work is either," suddenly occurred to him. Mr. Mounthead's work consisted mostly in a little bookkeeping, and in ordering people about. He only served in the shop as a kind of social relaxation. If he, Sam Meads, didn't serve in his shop himself all day from early morning till late evening, goodness knows what would happen to the business Besides-the pettiness of it all! Little bits of cheese, penny tins of mustard, string, weighing out sugar and biscuits, cutting bacon, measuring off ribbons and calico, and flannelette. People gossiping all day, and running up little accounts it was always hard to collect.

But here-oh, the snappy quick profit. Everybody paying on the nail, served in a second, and what a profit! Enough to buy a farm for a son as though it was an umbrella. Walking home, a little dejectedly, later on, he struck the road with his stick, and muttered:

"Damn that man!"

V

Mrs. James Mounthead was rather pleased with her starched ninon. She leant back luxuriously in the easy chair, yawned, and pressed her hands along the sides of her well-fitting skirt. Gilt bangles round her wrists rattled pleasantly during this performance. A paste star glittered on her ample bosom. She heard James moving ponderously on the landing below; the bar had closed. He came puffily up the stairs and opened the door.

"A nightcap, Queenie?" he wheezed through the creaking machinery of his respiratory organs.

Mrs. Mounthead smiled brightly. "I think I will to-night, Jim." He went to a cabinet and poured out two mixed drinks. He handed his wife one, and raising the other to his lips, said:

"Well, here's to the boy!"

"Here's to James the Second!" she replied, and drank deeply. Her eyes sparkled. Mrs. Mounthead was excited. The bangles clattered against the glass as she set it down.

"Come and give me a kiss, old dear," she said, leaning back.

Without making any great show of enthusiasm, James did as he was bidden. He, too, was a little excited, but his excitement was less amorous than commercial.

He had paid nearly twelve hundred pounds less for Bolder's farm than he had expected. The news of his purchase was all over the neighbourhood. It had impressed everyone. People looked at him differently.

He was becoming a big man, the big man in those parts.

He could buy another farm to-morrow, and it wouldn't break him. And the boy-the boy was a good boy; he would do well, too.

A little drink easily affected Mrs. Mounthead. She became garrulous.

"I had a good time at the Welfare, though some of the old cats didn't like me, I know. Ha, ha, ha, what do I care? We could buy the whole lot up if we wanted to, except perhaps the Wonnicots.

Mine was the only frock worth a tinker's cuss. Lord! You should have seen old Mrs. Meads! Looked like a washerwoman on a Sunday. The vicar was ever so nice. He called me madam, and said he 'oped I often come. I gave a fiver to the fund. Ha, ha, ha, I didn't tell 'em that I made it backing 'Ringcross 'for the Nunhead Stakes yesterday! They'd have died." During this verbal explosion, James Mounthead thoughtfully regarded his glass. And he thought to himself: "Um. It's a pity Queenie gives herself away sometimes." He didn't particularly want to hear about the Welfare.

He wanted to talk about "James the Second" and the plans for the future. He wanted to indulge in the luxury of talking about their success, but he didn't want to boast about wealth in quite that way.

He had queer ambitions not unconnected with the land he lived on. He had not always been in the licensing trade. His father had been a small landed proprietor and a stock breeder; a man of stern unrelenting principles. From his father he, James Mounthead, had inherited a kind of reverence for the ordered development of land and cattle, an innate respect for the sanctity of tradition, caste, property and fair dealing. His wife had always been in the licensing trade. She was the daughter of a publican at Pondhurst. As a girl she had served in the bar. All her relations were licensing people. When she had a little to drink-she was apt to display her worst side, to give herself away. James sighed.

"Did Mrs. Wonnicott say anything about her husband?" he asked, to change the subject.

"You bet she did. Tried to put it across us-when I told her about us buying Bolder's farm-said her old man had thought of bidding for it, but he knew it was poor in root crops and the soil was no good for corn, and that Sturge had neglected the place too long. The old cat! I said: 'Yes, and p'raps it wouldn't be convenient to pay for it just now, after 'aving bought a lawn mower!' Ha, ha, ha. He, he, he. O my!"

"I shouldn't have said that," mumbled Mr. Mounthead, who knew, however, that anything was better than one of Queenie's violent reactions to quarrelsomeness. "Come on, let's go and turn in, old girl." An hour later, James Mounthead was tossing restlessly between the sheets. Queenie's reference to the Wonnicotts had upset him. He could read between what she had said sufficiently to envisage a scene, which he himself deplored. Queenie, of course, had given herself away again to Mrs. Wonnicott. He knew that both the Wonnicotts despised her, and through her, him. He had probably as much "money as Lewis Wonnicott, if not more. He certainly had a more fluid and accumulative way of making it, but there the matter stopped. Wonnicott was a gentleman; his wife a lady.

He, James, might have been as much a gentleman as Wonnicott if circumstances had been different. Queenie could never be a lady in the sense that Mrs. Wonnicott was a lady. Wonnicott led the kind of life he would like to live-a gentleman farmer, with hunters, a little house property, and some sound vested interests; a man with a great knowledge of land, horses, finance and politics.

He loved Queenie in a queer enduring kind of way.

She had been loyal to him, and she satisfied most of his needs. She loved him, but he knew that he could never attain the goal of his vague ambitions, with her clinging to his heels. He thought of Lewis Wonnicott sleeping in his white panelled bedroom with chintz curtains and old furniture, and his wife in the adjoining room, where the bay window looked out on to the downs; and the heart of James became bitter with envy.

VI

"I don't think I shall attend those Welfare meetings any more," remarked Mrs. Lewis Wonnicott with a slight drawl. She gathered up her letters from the breakfast table and walked to the window.

In the garden below, Leach, the gardener, was experimenting with a new mower on the well-clipped lawns. The ramblers on the pergola were at their best.

Her husband in a broad check suit and a white stock, looked up from The Times and said:

"Oh, how is that, my dear?"

"They are getting such awful people in. That dreadful woman, the wife of Mounthead, the publican, has joined."

"Old Mounthead's all right-not a bad sort. He knows a gelding from a blood mare."

"That may be, but his wife is the limit. I happened to say something about the new mower, and she was simply rude. An awful vulgar person, wears spangles, and boasts about the money her husband makes out of selling whisky."

"By gad! I bet he does, too. I wouldn't mind I having a bit in his pub. Do you see Canadian Pacifies are still stagnant?"

"Lewis, I sometimes wish you wouldn't be so material. You think about nothing but money."

"Oh, come, my dear, I'm interested in a crowd of other things-things which I don't make money out of, too." "For instance?"

"The land, the people who work on it, horses, cattle, game, the best way to do things for everybody.

Besides, ain't I interested in the children? The two girls' careers at Bedales? Young Ralph at Rugby and going up to Cambridge next year?"

"You know they're there, but how much interest you take, I couldn't say."

"What is it you want me to do, my dear?"

"I think you might bestir yourself to get amongst better people. The girls will be leaving school soon and coming home. We know no one, no one at all in the neighbourhood."

"No one at all! Jeminy! Why we know everyone!"

"You spend all your time among horse-breeders and cattle-dealers, and people like Mounthead, and occasionally call on the Vicar, but who is there of any importance that we know?"

"Lord! What do you want? Do you want me to go and call at Crawshay Park, and ask Sir Septimus and Lady Letter to come and make up a four at bridge?"

"Don't be absurd! You know quite well that the Letters are entirely inaccessible. He's not only an M.P. and owner of half the newspapers in the country, but a millionaire. They entertain house parties of ministers and dukes, and even royalty. They can afford to ignore even the county people themselves. But there are others. We don't even know the county."

"Who, for instance?"

"Well, the Burnabys. You met St. John Burnaby at the Constitutional Club two or three times and yet you have never attempted to follow it up. They're very nice people and neighbours. And they have three boys all in the twenties, and the girl Sheila-she's just a year younger than Ralph."

"My word! Who's being material now?"

"It isn't material, it's just-thinking of the children."

"Women are wonderful," muttered Lewis Wonnicott into his white stock, without raising his head.

Mrs. Wonnicott swept to the door. Her thin lips were drawn in a firm straight line. Her refined hard little face appeared pinched and petulant. With her hand on the door-handle she said acidly:

"If you can spare half an hour from your grooms and pigs, I think you might at least do this to please me- call on Mrs. Burnaby to-day." And she went out of the room, shutting the door crisply.

"Oh, Jiminy-Piminy!" muttered Mr. Wonnicott.

"Jiminy-Piminy!" He stood up and shook himself. Then with feline intentness he walked quickly to the French window, and opening it walked down the steps into the garden.

All the way to the sunk rose-garden he kept repeating, "Jiminy-Piminy!" Once among the rose-bushes he lighted his pipe. (His wife objected to smoking in the house.) He blew clouds of tobacco smoke amongst imaginary green-fly.

Occasionally he would glance furtively out at the view across the downs. Half buried amongst the elms near Basted Old Church he could just see the five red gables of the Burnabys' capacious mansion.

"I can't do it," he thought, "I can't do it, and I shall have to do it." It was perfectly true he had been introduced to St. John Burnaby, and had spoken to him once or twice.

It was also true that Burnaby had never given any evidence of wishing to follow up the acquaintanceship.

Bit of a swell, Burnaby, connected with all sorts of people, member of half a dozen clubs, didn't race but went in for golf, and had a shooting box in Scotland. Some said he had political ambitions, and meant to try for Parliament at the next election. He didn't racket round in a check suit and a white stock and mix with grooms and farm hands; he kept up the flair of the gentleman, the big man, even in the country. He had two cars, and three acres of conservatory, and peacocks, and a son in the diplomatic service, a daughter married to a bishop. His wife, too, came of a poor but aristocratic family. Over at the "Five Gables" they kept nine gardeners and twenty odd servants. Everything was done tip-top.

Lewis Wonnicott turned and regarded his one old man gardener, trying the new mower, which Mrs. Mounthead had been so rude about to Dorothy. Poor Dorothy! She was touchy, that's what it was. Of course she did think of the children-no getting away from it. She was ambitious more for them than for herself or himself. She had given up being ambitious for him. He knew that she looked upon him as a slacker, a kind of cabbage. Well, perhaps he had been. He hadn't accomplished all he ought to. He had loved the land, the feel of horse-flesh, the smell of wet earth when the morning dews were on it. He had been a failure ... a failure.

He was not up to county people. He was unworthy of his dear wife's ambitions. Jiminy Piminy! It would be a squeeze to send Ralph up to Cambridge next year! He looked across the valley at the five red gables among the elms, and sighed.

"Lucky devil!" he murmured. "Damn it all! I suppose I must go."

VII

"You don't seem to realize the importance of it," said Gwendolen St. John Burnaby as her husband leant forward on his seat on the terrace, and tickled the ear of Jinks, the Airedale. "A career in the diplomatic service without influence is about as likely to be a success as a-as a performance on a violin behind a sound proof curtain. There's Lai, wasting his-his talents and genius at that wretched little embassy at Oporto, and all you've got to do is to drive three miles to Crawshay Park and put the matter before Sir Septimus."

"These things always seem so simple to women," answered Sir John, a little peevishly.

"Well, isn't it true? Do you deny that he has the power?"

"Of course he has power, my dear, but you may not realize the kind of life a man like that lives. Every minute of the day is filled up, all kinds of important things crowding each other out. He's always been friendly enough to me, and yet every time I meet him I have an idea he has forgotten who I am. He deals in movements in which men are only pawns. If I told him about Lai he would say yes, he would do what he could-make a note of it, and forget about it directly I turned my back." a Mrs. St. John Burnaby stamped her elegant Louis heels.

"Is nothing ever worth trying?"

"Don't be foolish, Gwen, haven't I tried? Haven't I ambition?" "For yourself, yes. I am thinking of Lal."
"Women always think of their sons before their husbands. He knows I've backed his party for all I'm
worth. He knows I'm standing for the constituency next time. When I get elected will be the
moment. I shall then have a tiny atom of power. For a man without even a vote in Parliament do you
think Letter is going to waste his time?"

"Obstinate!" muttered Mrs. Burnaby with metallic clearness. The little lines round the eyes and
mouth of a face that had once been beautiful became accentuated in the clear sunlight. The
constant stress of ambitious desires had quickened her vitality, but in the process had aged her body
before its time. She knew that her husband was ambitious, too, but there was always just that little
something he lacked in the great moments, just that little special effort that might have landed him
among the gods-or in the House of Lords.

He had been successful enough in a way. He had made money-a hundred thousand or so-in
brokerage and dealing indirectly in various manufactured commodities; but he had not even
attained a knighthood or a seat in Parliament. His heavy dark face betokened power and courage,
but not vision. He was indeed as she had said-obstinate. In minnow circles he might appear a triton,
but living within the same county as Sir Septimus Letter-Bah! About to leave him, her movement was
arrested by the approach of a butler followed by a gentleman in a check suit and a white stock,
looking self-conscious.

Mrs. St. John Burnaby raised her lorgnette. "One of these local people," she reflected.

On being announced the gentleman in the check suit exclaimed rapidly: "Excuse the liberty I take-
neighbours, don't you know. Remember me at the Constitutional, Mr. Burnaby? Thought I would
drop in and pay my respects." St. John Burnaby nodded.

"Oh, yes, yes, quite. I remember, Mr.—er—Mr."

"Wonnicott."

"Oh yes, of course. How do you do? My wife- Mr. Wonnicott." The wife and the Wonnicott bowed to
each other, and there was an uncomfortable pause. At last Mr. Wonnicott managed to say:

"We live over at Wimpstone, just across the valley—my wife, the girls are at school, boy's up at
Rugby."

"Oh yes-really?" This was Mrs. Burnaby, who was thinking to herself: "The man looks like a dog
fancier."

"Very good school," said St. John Burnaby. "Hot to-day, isn't it!"

"Yes, it's exceedingly warm."

"Do you golf?"

"No, I don't golf. I ride a bit."

"You must excuse me," said Mrs. St. John Burnaby, "I have to get a trunk call to London." She fluttered away across the terrace, and into the house. Mr. Wonnicott chatted away for several minutes, but St. John Burnaby was preoccupied and monosyllabic. The visitor was relieved to rescue his hat at last and make his escape. Walking down the drive he thought:

"It's no good. He dislikes me." As a matter of fact St. John Burnaby was not thinking about him at all. He was thinking of Sir Septimus Letter, the big man, the power he would have liked to have been. He ground his teeth and clenched his fists:

"Damn it!" he muttered, "I will not appeal for young Lai. Let him fight his own battles."

VIII

On a certain day that summer when the sun was at its highest in the heavens, Sir Septimus Letter stood by the bureau in his cool library and conversed with his private secretary.

Sir Septimus was wearing what appeared to be a ready-made navy serge suit and a low collar. His hands were thrust into his trouser pockets. The sallow face was heavily marked, the strangely restless eyes peered searchingly beneath dark brows which almost met in one continuous line. The chin was finely modelled, but not too strong. It was not indeed what is usually known as a strong face. It had power, but of the kind which has been mellowed by the friction of every human experience. It had alert intelligence, a penetrating absorption, above all things it indicated vision. The speech and the movements were incisive; the short wiry body a compact tissue of nervous energy.

He listened with the watchful intensity of a dog at a rabbit-hole. Through the door at the end of the room could be heard the distant click of many typewriters.

The secretary was saying:

"The third reading of the Nationalization of Paper Industries Bill comes on at five-thirty, sir. Boneham will be up, and I do not think you will be called till seven. You, will, of course, however, wish to hear what he has to say."

"I know what he'll say. You can cut that out, Roberts. Get Libby to give me a precis at six forty-five."

"Very good, sir. Then there will be time after the Associated News Service Board at four to see the minister with regard to this question of packing meetings in East Riding. Lord Lampreys said he would be pleased if I could fix an appointment. He has some information."

"Right. What line are Jennins and Castwell taking over this?"

"They're trying to side-track the issue. They have every un-associated newspaper in the North against you."

"H'm, h'm. Well, we've fought them before."

"Yes, sir. The pressure is going to be greater this time, but everyone has confidence you will get them down." The little man's eyes sparkled. "Roberts, get through on the private wire to- Lambe;

no, get through to all of them, and make it quite clear. This is not to be a party question. They're to work the unctuous rectitude stuff, you know-liberty of the subject and so on."

"Very good, sir. The car comes at one-fifteen.

You are lunching with Cranmer at Shorn Towers, the Canadian paper interests will be strongly represented there. I will be at Whitehall Court at three with the despatches. It would be advisable, if possible, to get Loeb of the finance committee. Oh, by the way, sir, I had to advise you from Loeb. They have received a cabled report of the expert's opinion from Labrador.

There are two distinct seams of coal on that land you bought in '07. A syndicate from Buffalo have made an offer. They offer a million and a quarter dollars down."

"What did we pay?"

"One hundred and twenty thousand."

"Don't sell."

"Very good, sir."

"Have you seen my wife, lately?"

"I have not seen Lady Letter for some days, sir.

I believe she is at Harrogate." The little man sighed, and drew out a cigarette case, opened it and offered one to Roberts, who accepted it with an elegant gesture. Then he snapped it to, and replaced it in his pocket.

"Damn it, Roberts, Reeves says I musn't smoke."

"Oh, dear!—only a temporary disability I trust, sir."

"Everything is temporary, Roberts." With his hands still in his pockets, he walked abstractedly out of the room. A little ormolu clock in the outer corridor indicated twenty minutes to one.

The car was due at one-fifteen. Thirty-five minutes: oh, to escape for only that brief period! Through the glass doors he could see his sister, talking to two men in golfing clothes, some of the house party. The house party was a perpetual condition at Crawshay. He turned sharply to the right, and went through a corridor leading out to the rear of the garage. He hurried along and escaped to a path between two tomato houses. In a few moments he was lost to sight. He passed through a shrubbery, and came to a clearing. Without slackening his pace, he walked across it, and got amongst some trees. The trees of Crawshay Park—his trees! ...

He looked up at the towering oaks and elms. Were they his trees-because he had bought them? They were there years before he was born. They would be there years after his death. He was only passing through them-a fugitive. "Everything is temporary, Roberts "Yes, even life itself. Jennins and Castwell! Of course they wanted to get him down! Were they the only ones? Does one struggle to the top without hurting others to get there? Does one get to the top without making enemies?

Does one get to the top without suffering, and bitterness, and remorse?

The park sloped down to a low stone wall, with an opening where one could obtain a glorious view across the weald of Sussex. The white ribbon of a road stretched away into infinity.

As he stood there, he saw a dark swarthy figure clamber down a bank, and stand hesitating in the middle of the road. He was a tramp with a stubbly red beard nearly concealing his face, and a filthy black green suit. In his hand he carried a red handkerchief containing his wordly belongings-a door-knob, a portion of a foot-rule, a tin mug stolen from a workhouse, some date stones, an onion, the shutter of a camera, and two empty match boxes.

Sir Septimus did not know this fact; he merely regarded the tramp as an abstraction. He observed him hesitate, exchange a word with a field labourer, look up at the sky, hunch his shoulders, and suddenly set out with long swinging strides down the white road.

Whither? There stirred within the breast of the millionaire a curious wistful longing. Oh, to be free! To be free! To walk across those hills without a care, without a responsibility. The figure, with its easy gait, fascinated him. The dark form became smaller and smaller, swallowed up in the immensity of nature. With a groan, Sir Septimus Letter buried his face in his hands and murmured:

"Lucky devil! ... lucky devil! 0 God! If I could die .... "

The Accident of Crime

I

Every seaman who makes the city of Bordeaux a port of call knows the Rue Lucien Faure. It is one of those irregular streets which one finds in the neighbourhood of docks in every city in the world.

Cord wainers, ships' stores, cafes and strange foreign eating houses jostle each other indiscriminately. At the further end of the Rue Lucien Faure, and facing Bassin a Flot No. 2, is a little cul-de-sac known as Place Duquesne, an obscure honeycomb of high dingy houses. It had often been pointed out to the authorities that the Place Duquesne was a scandal to the neighbourhood; not that the houses themselves were either better or. worse than those of adjoining streets, but that the inhabitants belonged almost entirely to the criminal classes. A murderer, an apache, a blackmailer, a coiner, hardly ever appeared in the Court of Justice without his habitation being traced to this unsavoury retreat.

And the authorities did nothing. Indeed Chief Inspector Tolozan, who had that neighbourhood under his special supervision, said that he preferred it as it was. He affirmed-not unreasonably-that it was better to have all one's birds in one nest rather than have them scattered all over the wood.

Tolozan, although a practical man, was something of a visionary. He was of that speculative turn of mind which revels in theories. The contemplation of crime moved him in somewhat the same way that a sunset will affect a landscape painter. He indulged in broad generalities, and it always gave him a mild thrill of pleasure when the actions or behaviour of his protegees substantiated his theories.

In a detached way, he had quite an affection for his "birds," as he called them. He knew their record, their characteristics, their tendencies, their present occupation, if any, their place of abode-which was generally the Place Duquesne. If old Granouz, the forger, moved from the attic in No. 17 to the basement in No. 11, Monsieur Tolozan would sense the reason of this change. And he never interfered until the last minute. He allowed Garros to work three months on that very ingenious plant for counterfeiting one franc notes. He waited till the plates were quite complete before he stepped in with his quiet:

"Now, mon brave, it distresses me to interfere ...." He admired the plates enormously, and in the van on the way to the police court he sighed many times, and ruminated upon what he called "the accident of crime." One of his pet theories was that no man was entirely criminal. Somewhere at some time it had all been just touch and go. With better fortune the facile Carros might now be the director of an insurance company, or perhaps an eminent pianist. Another saying of his, which he was very fond of repeating, was this:

"The law does not sit in judgment on people. Laws are only made for the protection of the citizen." His colleagues were inclined to laugh at "Papa Tolozan," as they called him, but they were bound to respect his thoroughness and conscientiousness, and they treated his passion for philosophic speculation as merely the harmless eccentricity of an urbane and charming character.

Perhaps in this attitude towards crime there have always been two schools of thought, the one which regards it-like Tolozan—as" the accident," the other, as represented by the forceful Muguet of the Council of Jurisprudence at Bayonne, who insists that crime is an ineradicable trait, an inheritance, a fate. In spite of their divergence of outlook these two were great friends, and many and long were the arguments they enjoyed over a glass of vermouth and seltzer at a quiet café "they sometimes favoured in the, Cours du Pave", when business brought them together. Muguet would invariably clinch the argument with a staccato:

"Well, come now, what about old Laissac?" Then he would slap his leg and laugh. Here, indeed, was a hard case. Here, indeed, was an irreconcilable, an intransigeant, an ingrained criminal, and as this story principally concerns old Laissac it may be as well to describe him a little in detail at once. He was at that time fifty-seven years of age. Twenty-one years and ten months of that period had been passed in penitentiaries, prisons and convict establishments. He was already an old man, but a wiry, energetic old man, with a battered face seamed by years of vicious dissipations and passions.

At the age of seventeen he had killed a Chinaman. The affair was the outcome of a dockside melee, and many contended that Laissac was not altogether responsible.

However, that may be, the examining magistrate at that time was of opinion that there had been rather too much of that sort of thing of late, and that an example must be made of someone.

Even the chink must be allowed some show of protection. Laissac was sent to a penitentiary for two years. He returned an avowed enemy of society.

Since that day, he had been convicted of burglary, larceny, passing of counterfeit coins, assault and drunkenness.

These were only the crimes of which he had actually been convicted, but everyone knew that they were only an infinitesimal fraction of the crimes of which he was guilty.

He was a cunning old man. He had bashed one of his pals and maimed him for life, and the man was afraid to give evidence against him. He had treated two women at least with almost unspeakable cruelty. There was no record of his ever having done a single action of kindliness or unselfishness.

He had, moreover, been a perverter and betrayer of others. He bred crime with malicious enjoyment. He trained young men in the tricks of the trade. He dealt in stolen property. He was a centre, a focus, of criminal activity. One evening, Muguet remarked to Tolozan, as they sipped their coffee:

"The law is too childish. That man has been working steadily all his life to destroy and pervert society. He has a diseased mind. Why arn't we allowed to do away with him? If, as you say, the laws were made to protect citizens, there's only one way to protect ourselves against a villain like Laissac- the guillotine." Tolozan shook his head slowly. "No, the law only allows capital punishment in the case of murder."

"I know that, my old cabbage. What I say is why should society bother to keep an old ruffian like that?" Tolozan did not answer, and Muguet continued:

"Where is he now?"

"He lives in an attic in the Place Duquesne, No. 33."

"Are you watching him?"

"Oh, yes."

"Been to call on him?"

"I was there yesterday."

"What was he doing?"

"Playing with a dog." Muguet slapped his leg, and threw back his head.

Playing with a dog! That was excellent! The greatest criminal in Bordeaux- playing with a dog! Muguet didn't know why it was so funny. Perhaps it was just the vision of his old friend, Tolozan, solemnly sitting there and announcing the fact that Laissac was playing with a dog, as though it were a matter of profound significance.

Tolozan looked slightly annoyed and added:

"He's very fond of dogs." This seemed to Muguet funnier still, and it was some moments before he could steady his voice to say:

"Well, I'm glad he's fond of something. Was there nothing you could lay your hands on?"

"Nothing." It is certainly true that Muguet had a strong case in old Laissac to confute his friend's theories. Where was "the accident of crime" in such a confirmed criminal? It is also true old Laissac was playing with a dog, and at that very moment. Whilst the representatives of law and order were discussing him in the Cafe" Basque he was tickling the ribs of his beloved Sancho, and saying:

"Up, soldier. Courage, my old warrior." Sancho was a strange forlorn-looking beast, not entirely retriever, not wholly poodle, indeed not necessarily dog at all. He had large sentimental eyes, and he worshipped his master with unquestioning adoration. When his master was out, as he frequently was on strange nocturnal adventures, he would lie on the mat by the door, his nostrils snuggled between his paws, and watch the door.

Directly his master entered the house, Sancho would be aware of it. He would utter one long whine of pleasure, and his skin would shake and tremble with excitement.

The reason of his perturbations this morning was that part of the chimney had fallen down with a crash. The brickwork had given way, and a little way up old Laissac could see a narrow opening, revealing the leads on the adjoining roof. It was summer time and such a disaster did not appal him unduly.

"Courage," he said," to-morrow that shall be set right.

To-day and to-night we have another omelette in the pan, old comrade. Tomorrow there will be ham bones for Sancho, and a nice bottle of fine champagne for the breadwinner, eh? Lie down, boy, that's only old Grognard!" The dog went into his comer, and a most strange looking old man entered the room. He had thin white hair, a narrow horse-like face with prominent eyes. His face appeared much too thin and small for the rest of his body, which had unexpected projections and convolutions.

From his movements it was immediately apparent that his left side was paralyzed. On the left breast of his shabby green coat was a medal for saving lives. The medal recorded that, at the age of twenty-six, he had plunged into the Garonne, and saved the lives of two boys. He sat down and produced a sheet of dirty paper.

"Everything is in order," he said dolefully.

"Good," said Laissac. "Show us the plan."

"This is the garage and the room above where you enter. The chauffeur left with Madame Delannelle and her maid for Pau this morning. They will be away three weeks or more. Monsieur Delannelle sleeps in this room on the first floor; but, as you know, he is a drug fiend.

From eleven o'clock till four in the morning he is in a coma. Lisette and the other maid sleep on the top floor.

Lisette will see that this other woman gets a little of the white powder in her cider before she retires. There is no one else in the house. There is no dog."

"It appears a modest enterprise."

"It is as easy as opening a bottle of white oil. The door of the room above the garage, connecting with the first landing in the house, is locked and the key taken away, but it is a very old-fashioned lock. You could open it with a bone toothpick, master."

"H'm. I suppose Lisette expects something out of this?" The old man sniggered, and blew his nose on a red handkerchief.

"She's doing it for love."

"You mean-young Leon Briteuil?"

"Yes, now this is the point, master. Are you going to crack this crib yourself, or would you like young Briteuil to go along? He's a promising lad, and he would be proud to be in a job with you."

"What stuff is there, there?"

"In the second drawer on the left-hand side in a bureau in the salon is a cash box, where Monsieur keeps the money from his rents. He owns a lot of small property.

There ought to be about ten thousand francs. Madame has taken most of her jewels, but there are a few trinkets in a jewel case in the bedroom. For the rest, there is a collection of old coins in a cabinet, some of them gold.

That is in the library, here, see? And the usual silver plate and trinkets scattered about the house. Altogether a useful haul, too much for one man to carry."

"Very well, I'll take the young-tell him to be at the Place du Pont, the other side of the river, at twelve-thirty.

If he fails or makes the slightest slip, I'll break his face. Tell him that. That's all."

"Right you are, master." Young Briteuil was not quite the lion-hearted person he liked to pose as, and this message frightened him.

Long before the fateful hour of the appointment, he was dreading the association of the infamous Laissac more than the hazardous adventure upon which he was committed. He would have rather made the attempt by himself. He was neat with his fingers and had been quite successful pilfering little articles from the big stores, but he had never yet experienced the thrill of housebreaking.

Moreover, he felt bitterly that the arrangement was unjust. It was he who had manoeuvred the whole field of operations, he with his spurious lovemaking to the middle-aged coquettish Lisette. There was a small fortune to be picked up, but because he was pledged to the gang of which Laissac was the chief, his award would probably amount to a capful of sous. Laissac had the handling of the loot, and he would say that it realized anything he fancied. Grognard had to have his commission also. The whole thing was grossly unfair. He deeply regretted that he had not kept the courting of Lisette a secret. Visions of unholy orgies danced before his eyes. However, there it was, and he had to make the best of it. He was politeness and humility itself when he met old Laissac at the corner of the Place du Pont punctually at the hour appointed. Laissac was in one of his sullen moods and they trudged in silence out to the northern suburb where the villa of Monsieur Delannelle was situated.

The night was reasonably dark and fine. As they got nearer and nearer to their destination, and Laissac became more and more unresponsive, the younger man's nerves began to get on edge. He was becoming distinctly jumpy, and, as people will in such a condition, he carried things to the opposite extreme. He pretended to be extremely light-hearted, and to treat the affair as a most trivial exploit. He even assumed an air of flippancy, but in this attitude he was not encouraged by his companion, who on more than one occasion told him to keep his ugly mouth shut.

"You won't be so merry when you get inside," he said.

"But there is no danger, no danger at all," laughed the young man unconvincingly.

"There's always danger in our job," growled Laissac.

"It's the things you don't expect that you've got to look out for. You can make every preparation, think of every eventuality, and then suddenly, presto! a bullet from some unknown quarter. The gendarmes may have had wind of it all the time. Monsieur Delannelle may not have indulged in his dope for once. He may be sitting up with a loaded gun. The girl Lisette may be an informer.

The other girl may have heard and given the game away. Madame and the chauffeur may return at any moment.

People have punctures sometimes. You can even get through the job and then be nabbed at the corner of the street, or the next morning, or the following week. There's a hundred things likely to give you away. Inspector Tolozan himself may be hiding in the garden with a half-dozen of his thick-necks. Don't you persuade yourself it's a soft thing, my white-livered cockerel." This speech did not raise Leon's spirits. When they reached the wall adjoining the garage, he was trembling like a leaf, and his teeth began to chatter.

"I could do with a nip of brandy," he said sullenly in a changed voice.

The old criminal looked at him contemptuously, and produced a flask from some mysterious pocket.

He took a swig, and then handed it to his companion. He allowed him a little gulp, and then snatched the flask away.

"Now, up you go," he said. Leon knew then that escape was impossible. Old Laissac held out his hands for him to rest his heel upon. He did so, and found himself jerked to the top of the wall. The old man scrambled up after him somehow. They then dropped down quietly on to some sacking in the corner of the yard. The garage and the house were in complete darkness.

The night was unnaturally still, the kind of night when every little sound becomes unduly magnified. Laissac regarded the dim structure of the garage with a professional eye. Leon was listening for sounds, and imagining eyes peering at them through the shutters ... perhaps a pistol or two already covering them. His heart was beating rapidly. He had never imagined it was going to be such a nerve racking business. Curse the old man! Why didn't he let him have his full whack at the brandy? A sudden temptation crept over him. The old man was peering forward. He would hit him suddenly on the back of the head and then bolt. Yes, he would. He knew he would never have the courage to force his way into that sinister place of unknown terrors. He would rather die out here in the yard.

"Come on," said Laissac, advancing cautiously towards the door of the garage.

Leon slunk behind him, watching for his opportunity.

He had no weapon, nothing but his hands, and he knew that in a struggle with Laissac he would probably be worsted. The tidy concrete floor of the yard held out no hope of promiscuous weapons. Once he thought: "I will strike him suddenly on the back of the head with all my might. As he falls I'll strike him again. When he's on the ground I'll kick his brains out...." To such a desperate pass can fear drive a man! Laissac stood by the wood frame of the garage door looking up and judging the best way to make an entrance of the window above. While he was doing so Leon stared round, and his eye alighted on a short dark object near the wall.

It was a piece of iron piping. He sidled towards it, and surreptitiously picked it up. At that exact instant Laissac glanced round at him abruptly and whispered:

"What are you doing?" Now must this desperate venture be brought to a head. He stumbled towards Laissac, mumbling vaguely:

"I thought this might be useful." Leon was left-handed and he gripped the iron piping in that hand. Laissac was facing him, and he must be put off his guard. He mumbled:

"What's the orders, master?" He doubtless hoped from this that Laissac would turn round and look up again. He made no allowance for that animal instinct of self-preservation which is most strongly marked in men of low mentality. Without a word old Laissac sprang at him. He wanted to scream with fear, but instead he struck wildly with the iron. He felt it hit something ineffectually. A blow on the face staggered him. In the agony of recovery he realized that his weapon had been wrenched from his hands! Now, indeed, he would scream, and rouse the neighbourhood to save him from this monster. If he could only get his voice! If he could only get his voice! Curse this old devil! Where is he? Spare me! Spare me! Oh, no, no ... oh, God! Old Laissac stuffed the body behind a bin where rubbish was put, in the corner of the yard. The struggle had been curiously silent and quick. The only sound had been the thud of the iron on his treacherous assistant's skull, a few low growls and blows. Fortunately, the young man had been too paralyzed with fear to call out. Laissac stood in the shadow of the wall and waited. Had the struggle attracted any attention? Would it be as well to abandon the enterprise? He thought it all out dispassionately. An owl, with a deep mellow note, sailed majestically away towards a neighbouring church. Perhaps it was rather foolish. If he were caught, and the body discovered that would be the end of Papa Laissac! That would be a great misfortune. Everyone would miss him so, and he still had life and fun in him. He laughed bitterly. Yes, perhaps he had better steal quietly away.

He moved over to the outer wall.

Then a strange revulsion came over him, perhaps a deep bitterness with life, or a gambler's lure. Perhaps it was only professional vanity. He had come here to burgle this villa, and he disliked being thwarted. Besides it was such a soft thing, all the dispositions so carefully laid.

He had already thought out the way to mount to the bedroom above the door. In half an hour he might be richer by many thousand francs, and he had been getting rather hard up of late. That young fool would be one less to pay. He shrugged his broad shoulders, and crept back to the garage door.

In ten minutes time he had not only entered the room above the garage but had forced the old-fashioned lock, and entered the passage connecting with the house. He was perfectly cool now, his senses keenly alert. He went down on his hands and knees and listened. He waited some time, focussing in his mind the exact disposition of the rooms as shown in the plan old Grognard had shown him. He crawled along the corridor like a large gorilla.

At the second door on the left he heard the heavy, stentorian breathing of a man inside the room. Monsieur Delannelle, good! It sounded like the breathing of a man under the influence of drugs or drink.

After that, with greater confidence, he made his way downstairs to the salon. With unerring precision he located the drawer in the bureau where the cash box was kept. The box was smaller than he expected and he decided to take it away rather than to indulge in the rather noisy business of forcing the lock. He slipped it into a sack. Guided by his electric torch, he made a rapid round of the reception rooms. He took most of the collection of old coins from the cabinet in the library and a few more silver trinkets. Young Briteuil would certainly have been useful carrying all this bulkier stuff. Rather unfortunate, but still it served the young fool right. He, Laissac, was not going to encumber himself with plate ... a few small and easily negotiable pieces were all he desired, sufficient to keep him in old brandy, and Sancho in succulent ham bones for a few months to come.

A modest and simple fellow, old Laissac.

The sack was soon sufficiently full. He paused by the table in the dining-room and helped himself to another swig of brandy, then he blinked his eyes. What else was there? Oh, yes, Grognard had said that there were a few of Madame's jewels in the jewel case. But that was in the bedroom where Monsieur Delannelle was sleeping, that was a different matter, and yet after all, perhaps, a pity not to have the jewels! H'm, Monsieur Delannelle was in one of his drug stumours. It must be about two o'clock. They said he never woke till five or six. Why not? Besides what was a drugged man? He couldn't give any trouble. If he tried to, Laissac could easily knock him over the head like he had young Briteuil-might just as well have those few extra jewels. His senses tingled rather more acutely as he once more crept upstairs. He pressed his ear to they keyhole of Monsieur Delannelle's bedroom. The master of the house was still sleeping.

He turned the handle quietly, listened, then stole into the room, closing the door after him. Now for it. He kept the play of his electric torch turned from the bed.

The sleeper was breathing in an ugly irregular way. He swept the light along the wall, and located the dressing-table-satinwood and silver fittings. A new piece of furniture-curse it! The top right-hand drawer was locked. And that was the drawer which the woman said contained the jewel case.

Dare he force the lock? Was it worth it? He had done very well. Why not clear off now? Madame had probably taken everything of worth.

He hesitated and looked in the direction of the sleeper.

Rich guzzling old pig! Why should he have all these comforts and luxuries whilst Laissac had to work hard and at such risk for his living? Be damned to him. He put down his sack and took a small steel tool out of his breast pocket. It was necessary to make a certain amount of noise, but after all the man in the bed wasn't much better than a corpse. Laissac went down on his knees and applied himself to his task.

The minutes passed. Confound it! It was a very obstinate lock. He was becoming quite immersed in its intricacy when something abruptly jarred his sensibilities.

It was a question of silence. The sleeper was no longer snoring or breathing violently. In fact he was making no noise at all. Laissac was aware of a queer tremor creeping down his spine for the first time that evening.

He was a fool not to have cleared out after taking the cash box. He had overdone it. The man in bed was awake and watching him! What was the best thing to do? Perhaps the fool had a revolver! If there was any trouble he must fight. He couldn't allow himself to be taken, with that body down below stuffed behind the dust-bin. Why didn't the tormentor call out or challenge him? Laissac crept lower and twisted his body into a crouching position.

By this action he saved his life, for there was a sudden blinding flash, and a bullet struck the dressing-table just at the place where his head had been. This snapping of the tension was almost a relief. It was a joy to revert to the primitive instincts of self-preservation. At the foot of the bed an eiderdown had fallen. Instinct drove him to snatch this up. He scrumpled it up into the rough form of a body and thrust it with his right hand over the end of the bed. Another bullet went through it and struck the dressing-table again. But as this happened, Laissac, who had crept to the left side of the bed sprang across it and gripped the sleeper's throat. The struggle was of momentary duration. The revolver dropped to the floor. The man addicted to drugs gasped, spluttered, then his frame shook violently and he crumpled into an inert mass upon the bed. A blind fury was upon Laissac.

He struck the still cold thing again and again, then a revulsion of terror came over him. He crouched in the darkness, sweating with fear.

"They'll get me this time," he thought. "Those shots must have been heard. Lisette, the other maid, the neighbours, the gendarmes ... two of these disgusting bodies to account for. I'd better leave the swag and clear." He drained the rest of the brandy and staggered uncertainly towards the door. The house was very still.

He turned the handle and went into the passage. Then one of those voices which were always directing his life said:

"Courage, old man, why leave the sack behind? You've worked for it. Besides, one might as well be hanged for a sheep as a lamb!" He went quietly back and picked up the sack. But his hands were shaking violently. As he was returning, the sack with its metallic contents struck the end of the brass bed. This little accident affected him fantastically.

He was all fingers and thumbs to-night. What was the matter? Was he losing his nerve? Getting old? Of course, the time must come when-God! What was that? He stood dead still by the jamb of the door. There was the sound of the stealthy tread on the stairs, the distinct creak of a board. How often in his life had he not imagined that! But there was no question about it to-night. He was completely unstrung.

"If there's another fight I won't be able to face it.

I'm done." An interminable interval of time passed, and then-that quiet creaking of another board, the person whoever it was, was getting nearer. He struggled desperately to hold himself together, to be prepared for one more struggle, even if it should be his last. Suddenly a whisper came down the stairs:

"Leon!" Leon! What did they mean? Eh? Oh, yes-Leon Briteuil! Of course that fool of a woman, the informer- Lisette. She thought it was Leon. Leon, her lover. He breathed more easily. Women have their uses and purposes after all. But he must be very circumspect.

There must be no screaming. She repeated:

"Leon, is that you." With a great effort he controlled his voice.

"It's all right. I'm Leon's friend. He's outside."

The woman gave a little gasp of astonishment.

"Oh! I did not know"

"Very quietly, mademoiselle. Compose yourself. I must now re-join him.

Everything is going well."

"But I would see him. I wish to see him to-night. He promised" Laissac hurried noiselessly down the stairs, thankful for the darkness. He waited till he had reached the landing below. Then he called up in a husky voice:

"Wait till ten minutes after I have left the house, mademoiselle, then come down. You will find your Leon waiting for you behind the dust-bin in the yard." And fortunately for Lisette's momentary peace of mind she could not see the inhuman grin which accompanied this remark.

From the moment of his uttering it till four hours later, when his mangled body was discovered by a gendarme on the pavement just below the window of the house in which he lived in the Place Duquesne, there is no definite record of old Laissac's movements or whereabouts.

It exists only in those realms of conjecture in which Monsieur Tolozan is so noted an explorer. Old Laissac had a genius for passing unnoticed. He could walk through the streets of Bordeaux in broad daylight with stolen clocks under each arm and it never occurred to anyone to suspect him, but when it came to travelling in the dark he was unique. At the inquest, which was held five days later, not a single witness could come forward and say that they had seen anything of him either that evening or night.

That highly eminent advocate, Maxim Colbert, president of the court, passed from the cool mortuary into the stuffy courthouse with a bored, preoccupied air. Dead bodies did not greatly interest him, and he had had too much experience of them to be nauseated by them-besides, an old criminal! It appeared to him a tedious and unnecessary waste of time. The old gentleman had something much more interesting occupying his mind. He was expecting his daughter-in-law to present his son with a child. The affair might happen now, any moment, indeed, it might already have happened. Any moment a message might come with the good tidings. A son! Of course it must be a son! The line of Colbert tracing their genealogy back to the reign of Louis XN must be perpetuated. A distinguished family of advocates, generals, rulers of men. A son! It annoyed him a little in that he suspected that his own son was anxious to have a daughter. Bah! Selfishness.

Let us see what is this 'case all about? Oh, yes, an old criminal named Theodore Laissac, aged fifty-seven, wanted by the police in connection with a mysterious crime at the villa of Monsieur and Madame Delannelle. The body found by a printer's devil, named Adolp Roger, at 4-15 a.m. on the morning of the ninth, on the pavement of the Place Duquesne. Witness informed police. Sub inspector Floquette attested to the finding of body as indicated by witness. The position of body directly under attic window, five stories high, occupied by deceased, suggesting that he had fallen or thrown himself therefrom.

Good! Quite clear. A life of crime, result-suicide. Will it be a boy or a girl? Let us have the deceased's record....

A tall square-bearded inspector stood up in the body of the court, and in a sepulchral voice read out the criminal life record of Theodore Laissac. It was not pretty reading.

It began at the age of seventeen with the murder of the Chinaman, Ching Loo, and from thence onward it revealed a deplorable story of villainy and depravity. The record of evil doings and the award of penalties became monotonous. The mind of Maxim Colbert wandered back to his son, and to his son's son. He had already seen the case in a nutshell and dismissed it. It would give him a pleasant opportunity a little later on. A homily on the wages of sin ... a man whose life was devoted to evildoing, in the end driven into a corner by the forces of justice, smitten by the demons of conscience, dies the coward's death. A homily on cowardice, quoting a passage from Thomas K Kempis, excellent! ... Would they send him a telegram? Or would the news come by hand? What was that the Counsel for the Right of the Poor was saying? Chief Inspector Tolozan wished to give evidence.

Ah, yes, why not? A worthy fellow, Inspector Tolozan.

He had known him for many years, worked with him on many cases, an admirable, energetic officer, a little given to theorizing-an interesting fellow, though. He would cross-examine him himself.

Inspector Tolozan took his place in the witness box, and bowed to the president. His steady grey eyes regarded the court thoughtfully as he tugged at his thin grey imperial.

"Now, Inspector Tolozan, I understand that you have this district in which this-unfortunate affair took place, under your own special supervision?"

"Yes, monsieur le president."

"You have heard the evidence of the witnesses Roger and Floquette with regard to the finding of the body?"

"Yes, monsieur."

"Afterwards, I understand, you made an inspection of the premises occupied by the deceased?"

"Yes, monsieur."

"At what time was that?" "At six-fifteen, monsieur."

"Did you arrive at any conclusions with regard to the cause or motive of the- er accident?"

"Yes, monsieur le president."

"What conclusions did you come to?"

"I came to the conclusion that the deceased, Theodore Laissac, met his death trying to save the life of a dog."

"A dog! Trying to save the life of a dog!"

III

"Yes, monsieur." The president looked at the court, the court looked at the president and shuffled with papers, glancing apprehensively at the witness between times. There was no doubt that old Tolozan was becoming cranky, very cranky indeed. The president cleared his throat-was he to be robbed of his homily on the wages of sin? "Indeed, Monsieur Tolozan, you came to the conclusion that the deceased met his death trying to save the life of a dog!

Will you please explain to the court how you came to these conclusions?"

"Yes, monsieur le president; the deceased had a dog to which he was very devoted."

"Wait one moment, Inspector Tolozan, how do you know that he was devoted to this dog?"

"I have seen him with it. Moreover, during the years he has been under my supervision he has always had a dog to which he was devoted. I could call some of his criminal associates to prove that although he was frequently cruel to men, women and even children, he would never strike or be unkind to a dog. He would never burgle a house guarded by a dog in case he had to use violence."

"Proceed."

"During that day or evening there had apparently been a slight subsidy in the chimney place of the attic occupied by Laissac. Some brickwork had collapsed, leaving a narrow aperture just room enough for a dog to squeeze its body through, and get out on the sloping leads of the house next door. The widow, Forbin, who occupies the adjoining attic, complains that she was kept awake for three hours that night by the whining of a dog on the leads above. This whining ceased about three-thirty, which must have been the time that the deceased met his death. There was only one way for a man to get from his attic to these leads and that was a rain-water pipe, sloping from below the window at an angle of forty-five degrees to the roof next door. He could stand on this water pipe, but there was nothing to cling to except small projections of brick till he could scramble hold of the gutter above. He never reached the gutter."

"All of this is pure conjecture, of course, Inspector Tolozan."

"Not entirely, monsieur le president. My theory is that after Laissac's departure, the dog became disconsolate and restless, as they often will, knowing by some mysterious instinct that its master was in danger. He tried to get out of the room and eventually succeeded in forcing his way through the narrow aperture in the fireplace. His struggle getting through brought down some more brickwork and closed up the opening. This fact I have verified. Out on the sloping roof the dog naturally became terrified. There was no visible means of escape; the roof was sloping, and the night cold. Moreover, he seemed more cut off from his master than ever. As the widow, Forbin, asserts, he whined pitiably. Laissac returned some time after three o'clock. He reached the attic. The first thing he missed was the dog. He ran to the window and heard it whining on the roof above. Probably he hesitated for some time as the best thing to do. The dog leaned over and saw him. He called to it to be quiet, but so agitated did it appear, hanging over the edge of that perilous slope, that Laissac thought every moment that it would jump.

Monsieur le president, nearly every crime has been lain at the door of the deceased, but he has never been accused of lack of physical courage. Moreover, he was accustomed to climbing about buildings. He dropped through that window and started to climb up."

"How do you know this?"

"I examined the water pipe carefully. The night was dry and there had not been rain for three days. Laissac had removed his boots. He knew that it would naturally be easier to walk along a pipe in his socks. There are the distinct marks of stockinged feet on the dusty pipes for nearly two metres of the journey. The body was bootless and the boots were found in the attic. But he was an old man for his age, and probably he had had an exhausting evening. He never quite reached the gutter."

"Are the marks on the gutter still there?"

"No, but I drew the attention of three of my subordinates to the fact, and they are prepared to support my view. It rained the next day. The body of the dog was found by the side of its master."

"Indeed! Do you suggest that the dog-committed suicide as it were?" Tolozan shrugged his shoulders and bowed. It was not his business to understand the psychology of dogs. He was merely giving evidence in support of his theories concerning the character of criminals-" birds "-and the accident of crime.

Maxim Colbert was delighted. The whole case had been salvaged from the limbo of dull routine. He even forgave Tolozan for causing him to jettison those platitudes upon the wages of sin. He had made it interesting. Besides, he felt in a good humour-it would surely be a boy! The procedure of the court bored him, but he was noticeably cheerful, almost gay. He thanked the inspector profusely for his evidence. Once he glanced at the clock casually, and said in an impressive voice:

"Perhaps we may say of the deceased-he lived a vicious life, but he died not ingloriously." The court broke up and he passed down into a quadrangle at the back where a pale sun filtered. Lawyers, ushers, court functionaries and police officials were scattering or talking in little groups. Standing outside a group he saw the spare figure of Inspector Tolozan. He touched his arm and smiled. "Well, my friend, you established an interesting case.

I feel that the verdict was just, and yet I cannot see that it in any way corroborates your theory of the accident of crime." Tolozan paused and blinked up at the sun.

"It did not corroborate perhaps, but it did nothing to" "Well? This old man was an inveterate criminal.

The fact that he loved a dog-it's not a very great commendation. Many criminals do."
"But they would not give their lives, monsieur. A man who would do that is capable of-I mean to say it was probably an accident that he was not a better man. "

"Possibly, possibly! But the record, my dear Tolozan!" "One may only conjecture."

"What is your conjecture?" Tolozan gazed dreamily up at the Gothic tracery of the adjoining chapel. Then he turned to Monsieur Colbert and said very earnestly:

"You must remember that there was nothing against Laissac until the age of seventeen. He had been a boy of good character. His father was an honest wheelwright.

At the age of seventeen the boy was to go to sea on the sailing ship La Turenne. Owing to some trouble with the customs authorities the sailing of the ship was delayed twenty-four hours.

The boy was given shore leave. He hung about the docks. There was nothing to do. He had no money to spend on entertainment. My conjecture is this. Let us suppose it was a day like this, calm and sunny with a certain quiet exhilaration in the air. Eh? The boy wanders around the quays and stares in the shops.

Suddenly at the corner of the Rue Bayard he peeps down into a narrow galley and beholds a sight which drives the blood wildly through his veins."

"What sight. Monsieur Tolozan?"

"The chinaman, Cheng Loo, being cruel to a dog."

"Ah! I see your implication."

"The boy sees red. There is the usual brawl and scuffle. He possibly does not realize his own strength.

Follow the lawcourt and the penitentiary. Can you not understand how such an eventuality would embitter him against society? To him in the hereafter the dog would stand as the symbol of patient suffering, humanity as the tyrant. He would be at war for ever, an outcast, a derelict.

He was raw, immature, uneducated. He was at the most receptive stage. His sense of justice was outraged. The penitentiary made him a criminal."

The Funny Man's Day

His round fat little face appeared seraphic in sleep. If only the hair were not greying at the temples and getting very, very thin on top, and the lines about the eyes and mouth becoming rather too accentuated, it might have been the head of one of Donatello's bambini. It was not until Mrs. Lamb, his ancient housekeeper, bustled into the room with a can and said: "Your water, Mr. Basingstoke"—the intrusion causing him to open his eyes-that it became apparent that he was a man past middle age. His eyes were very large "goose-gog eyes" the children called them. As elderly people will, it took him some few moments to focus his mentality. A child will wake up, and carry on from the exact instant it went to sleep; but it takes a middle-aged man or woman a moment or so to realize where they are, what day in the week it is, what happened yesterday, what is going to happen to-day, whether they are happy or not. Certainly with regard to the latter query there is always a subconscious pressure which warns them. Almost before they have decided which day in the week it is, a voice is whispering:

"Something occurred yesterday to make you unhappy," or" Things are going well. You are happy just now," and then the true realization of their affairs, and loves, and passions unfolds itself. They continue yesterday's story.

As to James Jasper Basingstoke, it was not his business to indulge in the slightest apprehension with regard to his condition of happiness or unhappiness.

He was a funny man. It was his profession, his mission, his natural gift. From early morning, when his housekeeper awakened him, till, playing with the children- all the children adored him-practising, interviewing managers and costumiers, dropping into the club and exchanging stories with some of the other "dear old boys," right on until he had finished his second show at night it was his mission to leave behind him a long trail of smiles and laughter. Consequently, he merely sat up in bed, blinked and called out:

"I am deeply indebted to your Lambship."

"Nibby's got hiccups," replied that lady, who was not unused to this term of address. Nibby was Mrs.

Lamb's grandson. His real name was Percy Alexander.

The granddaughter's name was Violetta Gladys, and she was known as Tibby. They lived next door. These names, of course, had been invented by the Funny Man, who lived in a world of make-believe, where no one at all was known by their real name.

He himself was known in the theatrical profession as "Willy Nilly."

"I am distressed to hear that," exclaimed Willy Nilly. "Hiccoughs at nine o'clock in the morning! You don't say so! I always looked upon it as a nocturnal disease. The result of too many hie, haec, hock cups."

"You must have your fun, Mr. Basingstoke, but the pore little feller has been very bad ever since he woke up." Willy Nilly leapt out of bed and rolled across to the chest of drawers. He there produced a bottle containing little white capsules, two of which he handed to Mrs. Lamb.

"Crunch these up and swallow with a little milk, then lie on his back and think of emerald green parrots flying above a dark forest, where monkeys are hanging by their tails. In our profession the distress of hiccoughs is quite prevalent and we always cure it in this way.

A man who can't conquer hiccoughs can never expect to top the bill. Now tell Master Nibby that, dear lady." Mrs. Lamb looked at the white capsules interestingly.

"Do you really mean that, Mr. Basingstoke?" The little fat man struck a dramatic situation. "Did you ever find me not a man of my word, Lady Lamb?"

"You are a one," replied the housekeeper, and retired, holding the capsules carefully balanced in the centre of her right palm, as though they contained some secret charm which she was fearful of dispelling by her contact.

The little fat man thrust out his arms in the similitude of some long-forgotten clumsy exercise. Then he regarded himself in the mirror.

"Not too thumbs up, old boy, not too thumbs up.

It's going, you know. All the Apollo beauty-oh, you little depraved ruffian, go and hold your head under the tap." No, no, it was not the business of Willy Nilly to be depressed by these reflections either in the mirror or upon the mind. He seized the strop suspended from a hook on the architrave of the window and began to flash his razor backwards and forwards whilst he sang:

"Oh, what care I for a new feather bed.

And a sheet turned down so bravely-O." The raggle-taggle gypsies accompanied him intermittently throughout the whole operation of shaving, including the slight cut just beneath the lobe of his left ear. The business of washing and dressing was no perfunctory performance with the Funny Man. He had a personality to sustain. Moreover, among the programme of activities for the day included attendance at a wedding. There is nothing at which a funny man can be so really funny as at a wedding. One funny man at least is almost essential for the success of this time-honoured ritual. And this was a very, very special wedding; the wedding of his two dearest and greatest friends, Katie Easebrook, the pretty comedienne, and Charlie Derrick, that most brilliant writer of ballads.

A swell affair it was to be in Clapham Parish Church, with afterwards a reception at the Hautboy Hotel- everything to be done "in the best slap-up style, old boy." No wonder Willy Nilly took an unconscionable time folding his voluminous black stock, adorned with the heavy gold pin, removing the bold check trousers from under the mattress, tugging at the crisp white waistcoat till it adopted itself indulgently to the curves of his figure, and hesitating for fully five minutes between the claims of seven different kinds of kid gloves. A man who tops the bill at even a suburban music hall cannot afford to neglect these things. It was fully three-quarters of an hour before he presented himself in the dining room below. Mrs. Lamb appeared automatically with the teapot and his one boiled egg.

"You'd hardly believe it," she said, "but Nibby took them white pills and his hiccups is abated."

"Ah! What did you expect, my good woman? Was Willy Nilly likely to deceive an innocent child? Did he think of emerald green parrots and a dark forest?"

"I told him what you said, Mr. Basingstoke. Here's the letters and the newspaper." The Funny Man's correspondence was always rather extensive, consisting for the most part of letters from unknown people commencing: "Dear Sir,—I wrote the enclosed words for a comic song last Sunday afternoon. I should think set to music you would make them very funny" or "Dear Sir, I had a good idea for a funny stunt for you. Why not sing a song dressed up as a curate called: 'The higher I aspire I espy her,' and every time you come to the word higher, you trip up over a piece of orange peel. I leave it to you about payment for this idea, but I may say I am in straitened circumstances, and my wife is expecting another next March." There was a certain surprising orderliness about the Funny Man's methods. Receipts were filed, accounts kept together and paid fairly regularly, suggestions and ideas were carefully considered, begging letters placed together, with a sigh," in case anything could be done a little later on, old boy." Occasionally would come a chatty letter from some old friend "on the road," or from his married sister in Yorkshire. But for the most part his correspondence was not of an intimate nature.

His newspaper this morning remained unopened.

The contemplation of his own programme for the day was too absorbing to fritter away nervous energy on public affairs. Whilst cracking the egg, he visualized his time-table. At ten o'clock, Chris Read was coming to try over new songs and stunts. At eleven-fifteen, he had an appointment with Albus, the costumier in Long Acre, to set the stamp of his approval upon the wig and nose for his new song: "I'm one of the Goo-goo boys." Katie and Charlie's wedding was at twelve-thirty and the wedding breakfast at "the Hautboy" at one-forty five. In the meantime, he must write two letters and manage to call on old Mrs. Labbory, his former landlady, who was very very ill. Poor old soul! She'd been a brick to him in the old days, when he was sometimes "out" for seven months in the year, out and penniless.

It was only fair now that he should help her a bit with the rent, and see that she had everything she needed.

Willy Nilly's life had been passed through an avenue of landladies, but the position of Mrs. Labbory was unique. He had been with her fifteen years and she was intimate with all his intimates.

At three-forty-five was a rehearsal with the Railham Empire orchestra. He must get that gag right where he bluffs the trombone player in his song: "Oh, my in-laws, my in-laws, why don't you leave me be." Perhaps a cup of tea somewhere, and then an appointment at five-fifteen with Welsh, to arrange terms about the renewal of contract. Knotty and difficult problems—contracts. Everyone trying to do you down-must have a clear head at five-fifteen. If there's time, perhaps pop into the club for half an hour, exchange stories with Jimmy Landish, or old Blakeney. A chop at six-thirty-giving him an hour before making-up for the first house. On at eight-twenty. Three songs and an encore-mustn't forget to speak to Hignet about that spotlight, the operator must have been drunk last night. Between shows interview a local pressman, and a young man who "wants to go on the stage, but has had no experience." Dash round for a sandwich and a refresher. On again at ten-twenty-five. Same three songs, same encore, same bluff on the trombone player.

Ten-fifty, all clear. Clean up and escape from the theatre if possible.

A last nightcap at the club, perhaps? Oh, but Bird Craft wanted him to toddle along to his rooms and hear a new song he had just acquired, "a real winner," Bird had said it was, about "The girl and the empty pram." Must stand by an old pal. Sometime during the day he must send two suits to be cleaned, and order some new underlinen. A beastly boring business, ordering vests and pants. He knew nothing about the qualities of materials-hosiers surely did him over that. Really a woman's business, women knew about these things.

Mrs. Lamb! No, not exactly Mrs. Lamb. He couldn't ask Mrs. Lamb to go and buy him vests and pants. A woman's business, a woman Heigho! Nearly ten o'clock already. Chris Read might arrive any minute. The Funny Man dashed downstairs and ran into the house next door. Tibby had already gone off to school, but Nibby had escaped, because at the moment of departure his attack of hiccoughs had reached its apotheosis. Now he was in trouble because it had left off, and his mother now declared he had been pretending. It took the Funny Man fifteen minutes to calm this family trouble. Nibby, putting it on! Nibby, playing the wag! Oh, come! Fie and for shame! Besides did Nibby's mother think that he, Dr. Willy Nilly, the eminent specialist of Harley Street, was a quack? Were his remedies spurious remedies? "Did you think of emerald green parrots in a dark wood, Nibby?"

"Yes."

"And monkeys hanging by their tails?"

"Yes."

"There, you see, Mrs. Munro! It was a genuine case, and a genuine cure."

"If he really had it, Mr. Basingstoke, I don't believe it was thinking about monkeys what cured him; it was them little white tabloids, and we thank you kindly."

"Mrs. Munro, here are two tickets for the Railham Empire for the first house to-morrow night. Come, and bring your husband, and then you will see that there are more people cured by thinking of monkeys hanging by their tails than there are by swallowing tabloids.

That is my business. I am a monkey hanging by its tail, and now I must be off. Goodbye, Nibby old boy.

Why, if this isn't a sixpence under the mat. Well, well, this is an age of miracles. No, you keep it, old boy.

Goodbye, Mrs. Munro. Come round and see me after the show to-morrow. Toot-a-loo, my dear." Chris was waiting on the doorstep, a fresh-complexioned young man inclined to corpulence. His face glowed with a kind of vacant geniality.

"Well, old boy, how goes it?"

"I've got a peach this morning, Willy old boy; I think you'll like it."

"Good boy, come on in."

The Funny Man's drawing-room was comfortably furnished with imitation Carolian furniture, a draped ottoman, and an upright Collard piano. The walls were covered with enlarged photographs of actors and actresses in gold and walnut frames, the majority of them were autographed and contained such inscriptions as: "To my dear old Willy, from yours devotedly, Cora,"

"To Uncle Nilly, one of the best, Jimmy Cotswold (The Blue Girl Company, Aug. 1899),"

"To Willy Nilly, 'my heart's afire,' Queenie," and so on.

"Now, let's see what you've got, old boy." Chris sat at the piano, and unwrapped a manuscript score.

"I think this ought to win out, old boy," he said.

"It's by Bert Shore. It's called' The Desert Island.' You see the point is this. You're a bit squiffy, old boy.

You see, red nose and battered top hat and your trousers turned up to the knees. You know how when it's been raining on a tarred road it looks like water.

Well, we have a set like that. It's really a street island-in Piccadilly, or somewhere. You're on it, and seeing all this shining water, you think you're on a desert island and the lamp-post's a palm tree. You take off your shoes and stockings and there's some good business touching the wet road with your bare toes. See, old boy? There's a thunderin' good tune. Listen to this- tum-te-too-te tum-te-tum, rum-te-too-te-tum-te-works up, you see to a kind of nautical air then gets back to the plaintive desert stuff- rum-tum-tum-rum-te-tum.

Then here's the chorus. Listen to this, old boy:

Lost in the jungle.
Oh, what a bungle,
Eaten by spiders and ants.

Where is my happy home? Why did they let me roam? Where are my Sunday pants? Good, eh? What do you think? Make something of it, old boy? Eh?"

The little man's eyes glowed with excitement. Oh, yes, this might assuredly be a winner. It was the kind of song that had made his reputation. The tune of the chorus was distinctly catchy, and his mind was already conceiving various business.

"Let's have a go at it, old boy," he said.

He leant over the other's shoulder and began to sing.

He threw back his head and thrust out his fat little stomach, his eyes rolled, and perspiration streamed down his face. He was really enjoying himself. He had just got to Lost in a jungle.

Oh, what a bungle.
Eaten by spiders and ants.

when there was a knock on the door, and Mrs. Lamb thrust her head in and said: "A telegram for you, Mr. Basingstoke."

"Eh? Oh! Well-er, never mind. Yes, thank you, my dear, give it to me." He opened the telegram absently, his mind still occupied with the song. When he had read it, he exclaimed:

"Good God! Poor old Joe! Yes, no, there's no answer, my dear. I must go out." Mrs. Lamb retired.

"Poor old Joe! Stranded, eh?"

"What is it, old boy?" said Chris.

"Telegram from Joe Bloom. He says: 'Can you wire me tenner, very urgent, stranded at Dundee?' Poor old Joe! He has no luck. He was out with 'The Queen of the Sea' company. They must have failed. Excuse me Chris, old boy." The Funny Man hurried out of the room and ran downstairs. He snatched up his hat and went out.

When he got round the corner, he ran. He ran as fast as he could to the High Street till he came to the London, City and Midland Bank. He filled up a cheque for fifteen pounds and cashed it. Then he ran out of the bank and trotted puffily across the road to the post office.

"I want to telegraph fifteen pounds, old girl," he said to the fair-haired lady behind the wires. Filling up the forms took an unconscionable time, and there all the while was poor old Joe stranded in Dundee perhaps without food! Dundee! Dundee of all places, a bleak unsympathetic town, hundreds of miles from civilization.

Well, that would help him out, anyway. True, he had had to do this twice before for Joe, and Joe had not, so far, paid him back, but Joe was a notoriously unlucky devil, and he, Willy Nilly, topping the bill at the Railham Empire, couldn't let a pal in.

When he got back to his own drawing-room, Chris was stretched at full length on the sofa, smoking a cigarette and drinking whisky and soda.

"Sorry to have kept you Chris, old boy."

"It's all right, Willy. I've just helped myself to a tot from the sideboard."

"That's right. That's right. Now let's see, it's a quarter to eleven. I'll have to wash out this trial, old boy. I shall be late for Albus. I like that song. I'd like to have another go at it. Have another tot, Chris, old boy. I'll join you, then I must be off." But he didn't get to Albus that morning, because on leaving the house he remembered that he hadn't called on old Mrs. Labbory. He must just pop in for a few moments. It was only ten minutes' walk away. He purchased a fowl and a bottle of Madeira and hurried to 27, Radnor Street. He found his old landlady propped up on the pillows, looking gaunt and distant, as though she were already regarding the manifestations of social life from a long way off and would never participate in them again.

"Well, Martha, old girl, how goes it? Merry and bright, eh? Oh, you're looking fine. More colour than last week, eh? ... eating better, old girl?" A voice came across the years.

"I'm not so well, Jim. God bless you for coming."

"Of course I come. I come because I'm a selfish old rascal. I come because I want to, I know where I'm appreciated, eh? Ha, ha, ha, now don't you think you're getting worse. You're getting on fine. We'll soon have you about again, turning out cupboards, hanging wallpapers. Jemimy! Do you remember hanging that convolvulus wallpaper in my bedroom in the Gosport Road, eh?" The Funny Man slapped his leg, and the tears rolled down his cheeks with laughter at the recollection of the episode.

"Do you remember how I helped you? And all I did was to step into a pail of size, nearly broke my leg, and spoilt the only pair of trousers I had! Ha, ha, ha! He, he, he! I had to go to bed for four hours while you washed them out and aired 'em. 0 dear!" Old Mrs. Labbory began to laugh, too, in a feeble distant manner. Then she stopped and looked at him wistfully.

"You going to Katie Easebrook's wedding, Jim?"

"Eh? Oh, yes, I'm going, old girl. I'm going straight on now." He hadn't meant to mention this. There's something a little crude in talking about a wedding to a dying woman. He paused and looked uncomfortably at his feet. The voice from the past reached him again.

"You ought to have married Katie Easebrook."

"Eh? What's that? Me? Oh, no, old girl, what are you talking about? Me marry Katie Easebrook? Why, I wouldn't have had the face to ask her. Not when there's a good fellow like Charlie about." Like some discerning oracle came the reply.

"Charlie's a good feller, a good-looking feller, too- but you would have made her a better husband, Jim."

With some curious twist of chivalry and affection the little man gripped the old woman's hand and kissed it.

"You've always thought too much of me, Martha, old girl."

"I've had good cause to, Jim .... Goodbye." He walked a little unsteadily down Radnor Street.

A pale October sun filtered through a light mist and gave to the meagre front gardens a certain glamour.

Fat spiders hung in glistening webs between the shrubs and Japanese anemones. Children were playing absorbing games with chalk and stones upon the pavement. Cats looked down sleepily from the security of narrow walls. He had to pat a little girl's head and arbitrate in a dispute between two girls and a boy regarding the laws of a game called" Snowball."

"Life is a lovely thing," he thought as he hurried on.

"Poor old Martha! ... She's going out." He was, of course, late for the service in the church.

In some way he did not regret this. He slipped quietly into a seat at the back, unobserved. A hymn was being sung, or was it a psalm? He didn't know. There was something about a church service he didn't like. It disturbed him at some uncomfortable level. Charlie was standing by the altar, looking self-conscious and impatient. Katie was a ghostly unrecognizable figure, like a fly bound up in a spool in a spider's web. Thirty or forty people were scattered on either side of the central aisle. He could only see their backs. The parson began to drone the service, slowly enunciating the prescribed purposes of the married state. Willy Nilly felt a flush of discomfort. It somehow didn't seem right that Katie should have to stand there before all these people and have things put to her quite so straight.

"Rather detailed, old boy," he thought. "Perhaps that's why a bride wears a veil." When it was over, he walked boldly up the aisle and followed a few intimates into the vestry. He was conscious of people indicating him with nudges and whispering: "Look! That's Willy Nilly!" In the vestry, Katie's mother was weeping, and Katie appeared to be weeping with one eye and laughing with the other. A few relatives were shaking hands, kissing and talking excitedly. Someone said: "Here's Willy Nilly." Charlie gripped his hand and whispered:

"Come on Willie, old boy, kiss the bride." The bride looked up at him with her glorious eyes, and held out her arms.

"Dear old Willie ... so glad you came, old boy." He kissed the bride all right, and held her from him. "God bless you, dear old girl. God bless you. May you ... may all your dreams come true, old girl." In most weddings there is a streak of pathos, but in theatrical weddings the note is predominant. It is as though the lookers on realize that these people whose life is passed in make-believe are bound to burn their fingers when they begin to touch reality. Perhaps their reactions are too violent to be bound within the four walls of a contract.

Katie's wedding certainly contained a large element of sadness.

"She looks so sweet and fragile. I hope he'll be good to her," women whispered.

The lunch at the Hautboy Hotel was hilarious to an almost artificial degree. A great deal of champagne was drunk, and toasts were prolific. It was here that Willy Nilly came in. The Funny Man excelled himself. He was among the people who knew him and loved him.

He made goo-goo eyes at the bridesmaids, he told stories, he imitated all the denizens of a farmyard, he gave a mock conjuring display, and his speech in proposing the health of the bride's father and mother was the hit of the afternoon. (He was not allowed the principal toast as that had been allocated to Charlie's father, who was a stockbroker.) To the waiter who hovered behind chairs with napkined magnums of champagne, he kept on saying:

"Not too much, old boy. I've a rehearsal at three-forty." Nevertheless, he drained his glass every time it was filled. The craving to be funny exceeded every other craving. Willy Nilly had knocked about the world in every kind of company. It took a lot to go to his head.

It was almost impossible to make him drunk. When at three o'clock it was time for the bride and bridegroom to depart he was not by any means drunk, certainly not so drunk as Charlie, but he was in a slightly detached comatose state of mind. He kissed the bride once more, and to Charlie he said:

"God bless you, old boy. Be good to her. You've got the dearest woman in the world." And Charlie replied:

"I know, old boy. You've been a brick to us. You oughtn't to have sent the cheque as well as all that silver. Good luck, old boy."

"O my in-laws, my in-laws, why don't you leave me be." It seemed but a flash from one experience to another, from pressing the girl's dainty shoulders in a parting embrace to stamping about on the draughty stage and calling into the void:

"Now, Mr. Prescott, I want a little more slowing down of this passage. Do you see what I mean, old boy? It gives me more time for the business." The gag with the trombone player was considerably improved. Must keep going, doing things a contract to sign at five-fifteen. He was feeling tired when the rehearsal was over-mustn't get tired before the two shows to-night. Perhaps he could get half an hour's nap after seeing the agent before it was time to feed.

Someone gave him a cup of tea in the theatre, and a dresser told him a long story about a disease which his wife's father got through sitting on a churchyard wall, waiting for the village "pub" to open at six.

There appeared no interval of time between this and sitting in front of the suave furtive-looking gentleman named Welsh who "handled" him on behalf of the United Varieties Agency. He was conscious of not being at his best with Welsh. He believed that he could have got much better terms in his new contract, but somehow the matter did not appear to him to be of great importance. He changed the subject and told Welsh the story about the sea captain and the Irish stewardess. Welsh laughed immoderately. After all, quite a good fellow-Welsh. He was anxious to get away and see some boys at the club. Jimmy would certainly have a new story ready. He hadn't seen Jimmy for four days.

Jimmy was certainly there, and not only Jimmy, but old Barrow, and Sam Lenning, and a host of others. He had a double Scotch whisky and proceeded to take a hand in the game of swapping improper stories. At one time something seemed to jog at his consciousness and say: "Do you really think much of this kind of thing, old boy?" And another voice replied: "What does it matter? ... They've just arrived at Brighton railway station. In another ten minutes they'll be at 'The Ship.'"

"I thought you were going to have a chop at six-thirty, Willy," someone remarked to him suddenly.

"So I am, old boy."

"It's seven-fifteen now." Good gracious! So it was! Well, he didn't particularly want a chop. He would have a couple of sandwiches and another double Scotch. He was quite himself again in his dressing room at the theatre. He loved the smell of grease paint and spirit gum, the contact of fantastic whiskers and clothes, the rather shabby mirror under a strong light. His first song was going to be "Old Fags," the feckless ruffian who picks up cigarette ends. The dresser, whose name was Flood and who always called him Mr. Nilly, was ready with his three changes.

"Number five's on," came the message down the corridors. Good! There was only "Charlemayne," the equilibrist, between him and "his people." Willy Nilly had got to love "his people" as he mentally designated them. He knew them, and they knew him-the reward of many years' hard work. He loved stumbling down the corridors, through the iron doors, and groping his way amidst the dim medley of the wings, where gorgeous unreal women, and men in bowler hats patted him as he passed and whispered:

"Hullo, Willy, old boy! Good luck!" He loved to wait there and hear his number go up; the roar of welcome which greeted it was music to his soul.

"Number seven!" The orchestra played the opening bars and then with a queer shuffle he was before them, a preposterous figure with a bright red nose, a miniature bowler hat, and a fearful old suit with ferns growing out of the seams, and a heavy sack slung across his back.

"Old Fags! Old Fags! See my collection of fine old fags. If you want to be happy.

If you want to be gay.
Empty your sack
At the fag-end of the day."

Oh, yes, you ought to see Willy Nilly in "Old Fags." The habitues at the Railham Empire will tell you all about him. The doleful wheezy voice, the quaint antics, and then the screamingly funny business when he empties the sack of cigarette ends all over the stage and, of course, at the bottom is a bottle of gin and a complete set of ladies' undies (apparently new and trimmed in pink). Then the business of finding innumerable cigarette ends in his unmanageable beard.

On that night, Willy Nilly was at his best. A lightning change and he came on as "The Carpet Salesman" in which he brought on a roll of carpet, the opportunities concerning which are obvious. Then followed "The lady who works for the lady next door." The inevitable encore-prepared for and expected followed. A terrible Russian-more whiskers, red this time-singing:

"O Mary-vitch, O Ada-vitch
I don't know which Ich lieber ditch;
I told your pa I'd got the itch;
He promptly hit me
On the snitch."

It was difficult for Willy to escape after this valiant satirical digression. He fled perspiring to his dressing-room.

"Give me a drink, old boy," he gasped to the lugubrious Flood.

He had smothered his face in cocoa-butter, when there was a knock on the door.

"Mr. Peter Wilberforce, representing the Railham Mercury."

"Ah, yes, come in, old boy." Mr. Wilberforce was in no hurry to depart. He had a spot-" just a couple of fingers, old boy" of whisky.

He wanted a column of bright stuff for the next issue of the weekly. "Is Railham behind the other suburbs in humour? Interview with the famous Willy Nilly—our local product."

"You just give me a lead," said Mr. Wilberforce, "I'll fill in the padding." Willy Nilly found turning out the bright stuff immediately after his performance the most exhausting experience of the day. He was quite relieved when, at the end of forty minutes, there was a knock at the door, and a woman with a lanky son were shown in. This was the young man who wanted to go on the stage.

The pressman departed and the mother started forth on a long harangue about what people said about her son's remarkable genius for acting. Before Willy Nilly knew where he was, he was listening to the boy giving imitations of Beerbohm Tree and Henry Ainley. It was quite easy to tell which was meant to be which, and so Willie grasped the young man's hand and said:

"Very good, old boy! Very good." He promised to do what he could, but by the time the mother had gone all over the same ground three times he found it was too late to pop round to the club again. It was nearly time to make up for the second show. He dozed in the chair for a few moments. Suddenly he thought:

"They've had dinner. They're probably taking a stroll on the front before turning in." He poured himself out another tot of whisky and picked up his red nose.

"O God! How tired I feel! ... Not quite the man you were, old boy." He found it a terrible effort to go on that second time. "Old Fags" seemed flat. He began to be subtly aware that the audience knew that he knew that the song wasn't really funny at all. At the end the applause was mild. "The Carpet Salesman" went even worse.

"Pull yourself together, old boy," he muttered as he staggered off. It wouldn't do. A man who tops the bill can't afford not to bring the house down with every song. He made a superhuman effort with "The lady who works for the lady next door." It certainly went better than the others, just well enough to take an encore rather quickly. On this occasion he altered his encore. Instead of" Mary-vitch," he sang a hilarious song with the refrain:

"O my I Hold me down! My wife's gone away till Monday!"

At the end of the first verse he felt that he had got them. Success excited him. He went for it for all he was worth. Willy Nilly was himself again. The house roared at him. He had the greatest difficulty in escaping without giving a further encore.

As he stumbled up the stone staircase to his dressing-room, he suddenly thought:

"They've gone to bed now." The imperturbable Flood followed him in, laden with properties.

"I'll just have one more spot, Flood, old boy." How tired he was! He cleaned up languidly and got into his normal clothes.

"Well, that's that, old boy," he said to Flood. "Now I think we'll toddle off to our bye-byes."

"Excuse me, Mr. Nilly, wasn't you going round to Mr. Bird Crafts?" Eh? Oh, yes, for sure; he'd forgotten about poor old Bird. Couldn't exactly let an old pal in. Well, he would have a cab and hang the expense-just stay a few minutes-dear old Bird would understand. But he stayed an hour at Bird Craft's. He listened to three new comic songs and a lot of patter.

"Yes, you've got a winner there, old boy," he remarked at the end of each song. It was nearly one o'clock when he groped his way up the dim staircase of his own house. The bedroom looked bleak and uninteresting. It had never struck him before in quite that way. He had always liked his bedroom with its heavy mahogany furniture and red plush curtains, but somehow to-night the place seemed forlorn ... as though something was terribly lacking.

"You're tired, old boy." He undressed and threw his clothes carelessly on chairs and tables. He got into bed and regarded the room, trying with his tired brain to think what was wrong. His clothes ought not to have been thrown about like that, of course. He felt that they and he were out of place in the large room. A strange feeling of melancholy crept over him.

"It's badly ordered ... it's all badly ordered, old boy." He had a great desire to cry, so weak he felt. But no, a man mustn't do that; a funny man certainly mustn't.

His mind wandered back to his old mother. He remembered the days when she had taught him to pray.

He would give anything for the relief of prayer. But he couldn't do that either, ft didn't seem exactly playing the game. He had put all that kind of thing by so long ago. He despised those people who lead unvirtuous lives and then in the end turned religious. He wasn't going to pretend. He turned out the light, and closed his eyes. He would neither weep nor pray, but he must express himself somehow. Perhaps he compromised between these two human frailties. Certainly his voice was very near a sob, and his accents vividly alive with prayer as he cried to the darkness:

"Charlie, old boy, be good to her .... For God's sake be good to her."

Old Fags

The boys called him "Old Fags," and the reason was not far to seek. He occupied a room in a block of tenements off Lisson Grove, bearing the somewhat grandiloquent title of Bolingbroke Buildings, and conspicuous among the many doubtful callings that occupied his time was one in which he issued forth with a deplorable old canvas sack, which, after a day's peregrination along the gutters, he would manage to partly fill with cigar and cigarette ends.

The exact means by which he managed to convert this patiently gathered garbage into the wherewithal to support his disreputable body nobody took the trouble to enquire.

Neither were their interests any further aroused by the disposal of the contents of the same sack when he returned with the gleanings of dustbins distributed thoughtfully at intervals along certain thoroughfares by a maternal borough council.

No one had ever penetrated to the inside of his room, but the general opinion in Bolingbroke Buildings was that he managed to live in a state of comfortable filth. And Mrs. Read, who lived in the room opposite, No. 477, with her four children, was of opinion that" Old Fags 'ad 'oarded up a bit." He certainly never seemed to be behind with the payment of the weekly three-and-sixpence that entitled him to the sole enjoyment of No. 475, and when the door was opened, among the curious blend of odours that issued forth, that of onions and other luxuries of this sort was undeniable.

Nevertheless, he was not a popular figure in the Buildings.

Many, in fact, looked upon him as a social blot on the Bolingbroke escutcheon. The inhabitants were mostly labourers and their wives, charwomen and lady helps, dressmakers' assistants, and several mechanics. There was a vague tentative effort among a great body of them to be a little respectable, and among some even to be clean.

No such uncomfortable considerations hampered the movements of Old Fags. He was frankly and ostentatiously a social derelict. He had no pride and no shame.

He shuffled out in the morning, his blotchy face covered with dirt and black hair, his threadbare green clothes tattered and in rags, the toes all too visible through his forlorn-looking boots. He was rather a large man with a fat, flabby person and a shiny face that was over-affable and bleary through a too constant attention to the gin bottle. He had a habit of ceaseless talk. He talked and chuckled to himself all the time, he talked to every one he met in an undercurrent of jeering affability. Sometimes he would retire to his room with a gin bottle for days together and then (the walls at Bolingbroke Buildings are not very thick) he would be heard to talk and chuckle and snore alternately, until the percolating atmosphere of stewed onions heralded the fact that Old Fags was shortly on the war-path again.

He would meet Mrs. Read with her children on the stairs and would mutter, "Oh, here we are again! All these dear little children been out for a walk, eh? Oh, these dear little children!" and he would pat one of them gaily on the head.

And Mrs. Read would say: "'Ere, you keep your filthy 'ands off my kids, you dirty old swine, or I'll catch you a swipe over the mouth!" And Old Fags would shuffle off muttering: "Oh, dear! Oh, dear! these dear little children! Oh, dear! Oh, dear!" And the boys would call after him and even throw orange peel and other things at him, but nothing seemed to disturb the serenity of Old Fags. Even when young Charlie Good threw a dead mouse that hit him on the chin he only said: "Oh, these boys! these boys!" Quarrels, noise and bad odours were the prevailing characteristics of Bolingbroke Buildings, and Old Fags though contributing in some degree to the latter quality, rode serenely through the other two in spite of multiform aggression. The penetrating intensity of his onion stews had driven two lodgers already from No. 476, and was again a source of aggravation to the present holders, old Mrs. Birdle and her daughter Minnie.

Minnie Birdle was what was known as a "tweeny" at a house in Hyde Park Square, but she lived at home. Her mistress-to whom she had never spoken, being engaged by the housekeeper-was Mrs. Bastien-Melland, a lady who owned a valuable collection of little dogs. These little dogs somehow gave Minnie an unfathomable sense of respectability. She loved to talk about them. She told Mrs. Read that her mistress paid "'undreds and 'undreds of pounds for each of them." They were taken out every day by a groom on two leads of five-ten highly groomed, bustling, yapping, snapping, vicious little luxuries. Some had won prizes at dog shows, and two men were engaged for the sole purpose of ministering to their creature comforts.

The consciousness of working in a house which furnished such an exhibition of festive cultivation brought into sharp relief the degrading social condition of her next room neighbour.

Minnie hated Old Fags with a bitter hatred. She even wrote to a firm of lawyers who represented some remote landlord and complained of" the dirty habits of the old drunken wretch next door." But she never received any answer to her complaint. It was known that Old Fags had lived there for seven years and paid his rent regularly.

Moreover, on one critical occasion, Mrs. Read, who had periods of rheumatic gout, and could not work, had got into hopeless financial straits, having reached the very limit of her borrowing capacity, and being three weeks in arrear with her rent, Old Fags had come over and had insisted on lending her fifteen shillings! Mrs. Read eventually paid it back, and the knowledge of the transaction further accentuated her animosity towards him.

One day Old Fags was returning from his dubious round and was passing through Hyde Park Square with his canvas bag slung over his back, when he ran into the cortege of little dogs under the control of Meads, the groom.

"Oh, dear! Oh, dear!" muttered Old Fags to himself "What dear little dogs! H'm! What dear little dogs!" A minute later Minnie Birdie ran up the area steps and gave Meads a bright smile.

"Good-night, Mr. Meads," she said.

Mr. Meads looked at her and said: "'Ullo! you off?"

"Yes!" she answered.

"Oh, well," he said," Good-night! Be good!" They both sniggered and Minnie hurried down the street.

Before she reached Lisson Grove Old Fags had caught her up.

"I say," he said, getting into her stride, "What dear little dogs those are! Oh, dear! what dear little dogs!" Minnie turned, and when she saw him her face flushed, and she said: "Oh, you go to hell!" with which unladylike expression she darted across the road and was lost to sight.

"Oh, these women!" said Old Fags to himself, "these women!" It often happened after that Old Fags' business carried him in the neighbourhood of Hyde park Square, and he ran into the little dogs. One day he even ventured to address Meads, and to congratulate him on the beauty of his canine proteges, an attention that elicited a very unsympathetic response, a response, in fact, that amounted to being told to "clear off." The incident of Old Fags running into this society was entirely accidental. It was due in part to the fact that the way lay through there to a tract of land in Paddington that Old Fags seemed to find peculiarly attractive. It was a neglected strip of ground by the railway that butted at one end on to a canal. It would have made quite a good siding but that it seemed somehow to have been overlooked by the railway company and to have become a dumping ground for tins and old refuse from the houses in the neighbourhood of Harrow Road. Old Fags would spend hours there alone with his canvas bag.

When winter came on there was a great wave of what the papers call "economic unrest." There were strikes in three great industries, a political upheaval, and a severe "tightening of the money market." All these misfortunes reacted on Bolingbroke Buildings. The dwellers became even more impecunious, and consequently more quarrelsome, more noisy and more malodorous. Rents were all in arrear, ejections were the order of the day, and borrowing became a tradition rather than an actuality. Want and hunger brooded over the dejected buildings. But still Old Fags came and went carrying his shameless gin and permeating the passages with his onion stews.

Old Mrs. Birdie became bedridden and the support of room No. 476 fell on the shoulders of Minnie. The wages of a "tweeny" are not excessive, and the way in which she managed to support herself and her invalid mother must have excited the wonder of the other dwellers in the building if they had not had more pressing affairs of their own to wonder about. Minnie was a short, sallow little thing, with a rather full figure, and heavy grey eyes that somehow conveyed a sense of sleeping passion. She had a certain instinct for dress, a knack of putting some trinket in the right place, and of always being neat.

Mrs. Bastien-Melland had one day asked who she was.

On being informed, her curiosity did not prompt her to push the matter further, and she did not speak to her, but the incident gave Minnie a better standing in the domestic household at Hyde Park Square. It was probably this attention that caused Meads, the head dog-groom, to cast an eye in her direction. It is certain that he did so, and, moreover, on a certain Thursday evening had taken her to a cinema performance in the Edgware Road. Such attention naturally gave rise to discussion and alas! to jealousy, for there was an under housemaid and even a lady's maid who were not impervious to the attentions of the good looking groom.

When Mrs. Bastien-Melland went to Egypt in January she only took three of the small dogs with her, for she could not be bothered with the society of a groom, and three dogs were as many as her two maids could spare time for after devoting their energies to Mrs. Bastien-Melland's toilette.

Consequently, Meads was left behind, and was held directly responsible for seven, five Chows and two Pekinese, or as he expressed it, "over a thousand pounds worth of dogs." It was a position of enormous responsibility. They had to be fed on the very best food, 'all carefully prepared and cooked and in small quantities. They had to be taken for regular exercise and washed in specially prepared condiments. Moreover, at the slightest symptom of indisposition he was to telephone to Sir Andrew Fossiter, the great veterinary specialist, in Hanover Square. It is not to be wondered at that Meads became a person of considerable standing and envy, and that little Minnie Birdle was intensely flattered when. he occasionally condescended to look in her direction. She had been in Mrs. Bastien Melland's service now for seven months, and the attentions of the dog-groom had not only been a matter of general observation for some time past, but had become a subject of reckless mirth and innuendo among the other servants.

One night she was hurrying home. Her mother had been rather worse than usual of late, and she was carrying a few scraps that the cook had given her. It was a wretched night and she was not feeling well herself, a mood of tired dejection possessed her. She crossed the drab street off Lisson Grove and as she reached the curb her eye lighted on Old Fags. He did not see her. He was walking along the gutter patting the road occasionally with his stick.

She had not spoken to him since the occasion we have mentioned. For once he was not talking: his eyes were fixed in listless apathy on the road. As he passed she caught the angle of his chin silhouetted against the window of a shop. For the rest of her walk the haunting vision of that chin beneath the drawn cheeks, and the brooding hopelessness of those sunken eyes, kept recurring to her.

Perhaps in some remote past he had been as good to look upon as Meads, the groom! Perhaps some one had cared for him! She tried to push this thought from her, but some chord in her nature seemed to have been awakened and to vibrate with an unaccountable sympathy towards this undesirable fellow-lodger.

She hurried home and in the night was ill. She could not go to Mrs. Melland's for three days and she wanted the money badly. When she got about again she was subject to fainting fits and sickness. On one such occasion, as she was going upstairs, at the Buildings, she felt faint, and leant against the wall just as Old Fags was going up. He stopped and said: "Hullo, now, what are we doing? Oh, dear!

Oh, dear!" and she said: "It's all light, old 'un.".

These were the kindest words she had ever spoken to Old Fags.

During the next month there were strange symptoms about Minnie Birdle that caused considerable comment, and there were occasions when old Mrs. Birdle pulled herself together and became the active partner and waited on Minnie. On one such occasion Old Fags came home late and, after drawing a cork, varied his usual programme of talking and snoring by singing in a maudlin key, and old Mrs. Birdle came banging at his door and shrieked out:

"Stop your row, you old. My daughter is ill. Can't you hear?" And Old Fags came to his door and blinked at her and said: "Ill, is she? Oh, dear! Oh, dear I Would she like some stew, eh?" And old Mrs. Birdle said: "No, she don't want any of your muck," and bundled back. But they did not hear any more of Old Fags that night or any other night when Minnie came home queer.

Early in March Minnie got the sack from Hyde Park Square. Mrs. Melland was still away, having decided to winter in Rome; but the housekeeper assumed the responsibility of this action, and in writing to Mrs. Melland justified the course she had taken by saying that "she could not expect the other maids to work in the same house with an unmarried girl in that condition." Mrs. Melland, whose letter in reply was full of the serious illness of poor little Anisette (one of the Chows), that she had suffered in Egypt on account of a maid giving it too much rice with its boned chicken, and how much better it had been in Rome under the treatment of Dr. Lascati, made no special reference to the question of Minnie Birdle, only saying that "she was so sorry if Mrs. Bellingham was having trouble with these tiresome servants." The spring came and the summer, and the two inhabitants of Room 4 76 eked out their miserable existence.

One day Minnie would pull herself together and get a day's charing, and occasionally Mrs. Birdle would struggle along to a laundry in Maida Vale where a benevolent proprietress would pay her one shilling and threepence to do a day's ironing, for the old lady was rather neat with her hands.

And once when things were very desperate the brother of a nephew from Walthamstow turned up.

He was a small cabinet maker by trade, and he agreed to allow them three shillings a week "till things righted themselves a bit." But nothing was seen of Meads, the groom. One night Minnie was rather worse and the idea occurred to her that she would like to send a message to him. It was right that he should know. He had made no attempt to see her since she had left Mrs. Melland's service. She lay awake thinking of him and wondering how she could send a message, when she suddenly thought of Old Fags. He had been quiet of late; whether the demand for cigarette ends was abating and he could not afford the luxuries that their disposal seemed to supply, or whether he was keeping quiet for any ulterior reason she was not able to determine.

In the morning she sent her mother across to ask him if he would "oblige by calling at Hyde Park Square and asking Mr. Meads if he would oblige by calling at 476, Bolingbroke Buildings to see Miss Birdle." There is no record of how Old Fags delivered this message, but it is known that that same afternoon Mr. Meads did call. He left about three-thirty in a great state of perturbation and in a very bad temper. He passed Old Fags on the stairs, and the only comment he made was: "I never have any luck! God help me!" and he did not return, although he had apparently promised to do so.

In a few weeks' time the position of the occupants of Room 476 became desperate. It was, in fact, a desperate time all round. Work was scarce and money scarcer.

Waves of ill-temper and depression swept Bolingbroke Buildings. Mrs. Read had gone-heaven knows where.

Even Old Fags seemed at the end of his tether. True, he still managed to secure his inevitable bottle, but the stews became scarcer and less potent. All Mrs. Birdle's time and energy were taken up in nursing Minnie, and the two somehow existed on the money now increased to four shillings a week, which the sympathetic cabinet maker from Walthamstow allowed them. The question of rent was shelved. Four shillings a week for two people means ceaseless gnawing hunger. The widow and her daughter lost pride and hope, and further messages to Mr. Meads failed to elicit any response. The widow became so desperate that she even asked Old Fags one night if he could spare a little stew for her daughter who was starving.

The pungent odour of the hot food was too much for her.

Old Fags came to the door.

"Oh, dear! Oh, dear!" he said, "What trouble there is! Let's see what we can do!" He messed about for some time and then took it across to them. It was a strange concoction. Meat that it would have been difficult to know what to ask for at the butcher's, and many bones, but the onions seemed to pull it together.

To anyone starving it was good. After that it became a sort of established thing-whenever Old Fags had a stew he sent some over to the widow and daughter. But apparently things were not doing too well in the cigarette end trade, for the stews became more and more intermittent, and sometimes were desperately "bony." And then one night a terrible climax was reached. Old Fags was awakened in the night by fearful screams. There was a district nurse in the next room, and also a student from a great hospital. No one knows how it all · affected Old Fags. He went out at a very unusual hour in the early morning, and seemed more garrulous and meandering in his speech.

He stopped the widow in the passage and mumbled incomprehensible solicitude. Minnie was very ill for three days, but she recovered, faced by the insoluble proposition of feeding three mouths instead of two, and two of them requiring enormous quantities of milk.

This terrible crisis brought out many good qualities in various people. The cabinet maker sent ten shillings extra and others came forward as though driven by some race instinct. Old Fags disappeared for ten days after that. It was owing to an unfortunate incident in Hyde Park when he insisted on sleeping on a flower bed with a gin-bottle under his left arm, and on account of the uncompromising attitude that he took up towards a policeman in the matter. When he returned things were assuming their normal course. Mrs. Birdle's greeting was:

"Ullo, old 'un, we've missed your stoos." But Old Fags had undoubtedly secured a more stable position in the eyes of the Birdles, and one day he was even allowed to see the baby.

He talked to it from the door. "Oh, dear! Oh, dear!" he said. "What a beautiful little baby! What a dear little baby! Oh, dear! Oh, dear!" The baby shrieked with unrestrained terror at sight of him, but that night some more stew was sent in.

Then the autumn came on. People whose romantic instincts had been touched at the arrival of the child gradually lost interest and fell away. The cabinet maker from Walthamstow wrote a long letter saying that after next week the payment of the four shillings would have to stop. He "hoped he had been of some help in their trouble, but that things were going on all right now. Of course he had to think of his own family first," and so on.

The lawyers of the remote landlord, who was assiduously killing stags in Scotland, "regretted that their client could not see his way to allow any further delay in the matter of the payment of rent due." The position of the Birdle family became once more desperate. Old Mrs. Birdle had become frailer, and though Minnie could now get about she found work difficult to obtain, owing to people's demand for a character from the last place. Their thoughts once more reverted to Meads, and Minnie lay in wait for him one morning as he was taking the dogs out. There was a very trying scene ending in a very vulgar quarrel, and Minnie came home and cried all the rest of the day and through half the night. Old Fags' stews became scarcer and less palatable. He, too, seemed in dire straits.

We now come to an incident that we are ashamed to say owes its inception to the effect of alcohol.

It was a wretched morning in late October, bleak and foggy. The blue-grey corridors of Bolingbroke Buildings seemed to exude damp. The strident voices of the unkempt children quarrelling in the courtyard below permeated the whole Buildings. The strange odour that was its characteristic lay upon it like the foul breath of some evil God. All its inhabitants seemed hungry, wretched and vile.

Their lives of constant protest seemed for the moment lulled to a sullen indifference, whilst they huddled behind their gloomy doors and listened to the rancorous railings of their offspring.

The widow Birdle and her daughter sat silently in their room. The child was asleep. It had had its milk, and it would have to have its milk whatever happened. The crumbs from the bread the women had had at breakfast lay ungathered on the bare table. They were both hungry and very desperate.

There was a knock at the door.

Minnie went to it, and there stood Old Fags. He leered at them meekly and under his arm carried a gin-bottle three parts full.

"Oh, dear! Oh, dear!" he said. "What a dreadful day! What a dreadful day! Will you have a little drop of gin to comfort you? Now! What do you say?" Minnie looked at her mother; in other days the door would have been slammed in his face, but Old Fags had certainly been kind in the matter of the stews. They asked him to sit down. Then old Mrs. Birdle did accept "just a tiny drop" of gin, and they both persuaded Minnie to have a little. Now neither of the women had had food of any worth for days, and the gin went straight to their heads. It was already in Old Fags' head firmly established.

The three immediately became garrulous. They all talked volubly and intimately. The women railed Old Fags about his dirt, but allowed that he had "a good 'eart." They talked longingly and lovingly about his "stoos," and Old Fags said:

"Well, my dears, you shall have the finest stoo you've ever had in your lives to-night." He repeated this nine times, only each time the whole sentence sounded like one word. Then the conversation drifted to the child, and the hard lot of parents, and by a natural sequence to Meads, its father.

Meads was discussed with considerable bitterness, and the constant reiteration of the threat by the women that they meant "to 'ave the lor on 'im all right," mingled with the jeering sophistries of Old Fags on the "genalman's behaviour," and the impossibility of expecting "a dog-groom to be sportsman," lasted a considerable time.

Old Fags talked expansively about" leaving it to him," and somehow as he stood there with his large puffy figure looming up in the dimly lighted room, and waving his long arms, he appeared to the women a figure of portentous significance. He typified powers they had not dreamt of.

Under the veneer of his hide-bound depravity Minnie seemed to detect some slow-moving force trying to assert itself. He meandered on in a vague monologue, using terms and expressions they did not know the meaning of.

He gave the impression of some fettered animal launching a fierce indictment against the fact of its life. At last he took up the gin-bottle and moved to the door and then leered round the room. "You shall have the finest stoo you've ever had in your life to-night, my dears!" He repeated this seven times again and then went heavily out.

That afternoon a very amazing fact was observed by several inhabitants of Bolingbroke Buildings. Old Fags washed his face! He went out about three o'clock without his sack. His face had certainly been cleaned up and his clothes seemed in some mysterious fashion to hold together.

He went across Lisson Grove and made for Hyde Park Square. He hung about for nearly an hour at the corner, and then he saw a man come up the area steps of a house on the south side and walk rapidly away. Old Fags followed him. He took a turning sharp to the left through a mews and entered a narrow street at the end. There he entered a deserted-looking "pub" kept by an ex-butler and his wife. He passed right through to a room at the back and called for some beer. Before it was brought Old Fags was seated at the next table ordering gin.

"Dear, oh dear! what a wretched day!" said Old Fags.

The groom grunted assent. But Old Fags was not to be put off by mere indifference. He broke ground on one or two subjects that interested the groom, one subject in particular being dog. He seemed to have a profound knowledge of dog, and before Mr. Meads quite realized what was happening he was trying gin in his beer at Old Fags' expense. The groom was feeling particularly morose that afternoon. His luck seemed out. Bookmakers had appropriated several half-crowns that he sorely begrudged, and he had other expenses. The beer-gin mixture comforted him, and the rambling eloquence of the old fool who seemed disposed to be content paying for drinks and talking, fitted in with his mood.

They drank and talked for a full hour, and at length got to a subject that all men get to sooner or later if they drink and talk long enough–the subject of woman. Mr. Meads became confiding and philosophic. He talked of women in general and what triumphs and adventures he had had among them in particular. But what a trial and tribulation they had been to him in spite of all. Old Fags winked knowingly and was splendidly comprehensive and tolerant of Meads' peccadillos.

"It's all a game," said Meads.

'You've got to manage 'em. There ain't much I don't know, old bird!"

Then suddenly Old Fags leaned forward in the dark room and said:

"No, Mr. Meads, but you ought to play the game you know. Oh, dear, yes!"

"What do you mean, Mister Meads?" said that gentleman sharply.

"Minnie Birdle, eh? you haven't mentioned Minnie Birdle yet!" said Old Fags.

"What the devil are you talking about?" said Meads drunkenly.

"She's starving," said Old Fags, "starving, wretched, alone with her old mother and your child. Oh, dear! yes, it's terrible!" Meads' eyes flashed with a sullen frenzy but fear was gnawing at his heart, and he felt more disposed to placate this mysterious old man than to quarrel with him.

"I tell you I have no luck," he said after a pause. Old Fags looked at him gloomily and ordered some more gin.

When it was brought he said:

"You ought to play the game, you know, Mr. Meads- after all-luck? Oh, dear! Oh, dear! Would you rather be the woman? Five shillings a week you know would"

"No, I'm damned if I do!" cried Meads fiercely. "It's all right for all these women. Gawd! How do I know if it's true? Look here, old bird, do you know I'm already done in for two five bobs a week, eh?

One up in Norfolk and the other at Enfield. Ten shillings a week of my money goes to these blasted women. No fear, no more, I'm through with it!"

"Oh, dear! Oh, dear!" said Old Fags, and he moved a little further into the shadow of the room and watched the groom out of the depths of his sunken eyes. But Meads' courage was now fortified by the fumes of a large quantity of fiery alcohol, and he spoke witheringly of women in general and seemed disposed to quarrel if Old Fags disputed his right to place them in the position that Meads considered their right and natural position. But Old Fags gave no evidence of taking up the challenge: on the contrary he seemed to suddenly shift his ground. He grinned and leered and nodded at Meads' string of coarse sophistry, and suddenly he touched him on the arm and looked round the room and said very confidentially:

"Oh, dear! yes, Mr. Meads. Don't take too much to heart what I said." And then he sniffed and whispered:

"I could put you on to a very nice thing, Mr. Meads.

I could introduce you to a lady I know would take a fancy to you, and you to her. Oh, dear, yes!" Meads pricked up his ears like a fox-terrier and his small eyes glittered.

"Oh!" he said. "Are you one of those, eh, old bird? Who is she?" Old Fags took out a piece of paper and fumbled with a pencil. He then wrote down a name and address somewhere at Shepherd's Bush.

"What's a good time to call?" said Meads. "Between six and seven," answered Old Fags.

"Oh, hell!" said Meads, "I can't do it. I've got to get back and take the dogs out at half-past five, old bird.

From half-past five to half-past six. The missus is back, she'll kick up a hell of a row."" Oh, dear! Oh, dear!" said Old Fags. "What a pity! The young lady is going away, too!" He thought for a moment, and then an idea seemed to strike him.

"Look here, would you like me to meet you and take the dogs round the park till you return?"

"What!" said Meads. "Trust you with a thousand pounds' worth of dogs! Not much!"

"No, no, of course not, I hadn't thought of that!" said Old Fags humbly. Meads looked at him, and it is very difficult to tell what it was about the old man that gave him a sudden feeling of complete trust. The ingenuity of his speech, the ingratiating confidence that a mixture of beer-gin gives, tempered by the knowledge that famous pedigree Pekinese would be almost impossible to dispose of, perhaps it was a combination of these motives. In any case a riotous impulse drove him to fall in with Old Fags' suggestion, and he made the appointment for half-past five.

Evening had fallen early, and a fine rain was driving in fitful gusts when the two met at the corner of Hyde Park.

There were ten little dogs on their lead, and Meads with a cap pulled close over his eyes.

"Oh, dear! Oh, dear!" cried Old Fags as he approached.

"What dear little dogs! What dear little dogs!" Meads handed the lead over to Old Fags, and asked more precise instructions of the way to get to the address.

"What are you wearing that canvas sack inside your coat for, old bird, eh?" asked Meads, when these instructions had been given.

"Oh, my dear sir," said Old Fags, "If you had the asthma like I get it, and no underclothes on these damp days! Oh, dear! Oh, dear!" He wheezed drearily and Meads gave him one or two more exhortations about the extreme care and tact he was to observe.

"Be very careful with that little Chow on the left lead. 'E's got his coat on, see? 'E's 'ad a chill and you must keep 'im on the move. Gently, see?"

"Oh, dear! Oh, dear! Poor little chap! What's his name?" said Old Fags. "Pelleas," answered Mr. Meads.

"Oh, poor little Pelleas! Poor little Pelleas! Come along ....You won't be too long, Mr. Meads, will you?"

"You bet I won't," said the groom, and nodding he crossed the road rapidly and mounting a Shepherd's Bush motor-bus he set out on his journey to an address that didn't exist.

Old Fags ambled slowly round the Park, snuffling and talking to the dogs. He gauged the time when Meads would be somewhere about Queen's Road, then he ambled slowly back to the point from which he had started. With extreme care he piloted the small army across the high road and led them in the direction of Paddington. He drifted with leisurely confidence through a maze of small streets. Several people stopped and looked at the dogs, and the boys barked and mimicked them, but nobody took the trouble to look at Old Fags. At length he came to a district where their presence seemed more conspicuous.

Rows of squalid houses and advertisement hoardings. He slightly increased his pace, and a very stout policeman standing outside a funeral furnishers' glanced at him with a vague suspicion.

However, in strict accordance with an ingrained officialism that hates to act "without instructions," he let the cortege pass. Old Fags wandered through a wretched street that seemed entirely peopled by children.

Several of them came up and followed the dogs.

"Dear little dogs, aren't they? Oh my, yes, dear little dogs!" he said to the children. At last he reached a broad gloomy thoroughfare with low irregular buildings on one side, and an interminable length of hoardings on the other that screened a strip of land by the railway- land that harboured a wilderness of tins and garbage.

Old Fags led the dogs along by the hoarding. It was very dark. Three children, who had been following, tired of the pastime, had drifted away. He went along once more.

There was a gap in a hoarding on which was notified that "Pogram's Landaulettes could be hired for the evening at an inclusive fee of two guineas. Telephone, 4 7901 Mayfair." The meagre light from a street lamp thirty yards away revealed a colossal coloured picture of a very beautiful young man and woman stepping out of a car and entering a gorgeous restaurant, having evidently just enjoyed the advantage of this peerless luxury. Old Fags went on another forty yards and then returned. There was no one in sight.

"Oh, dear little dogs," he said. "Oh, dear! Oh, dear! What dear little dogs! Just through here, my pretty pets. Gently, Pelleas! Gently, very gently! There, there, there! Oh, what dear little dogs!" He stumbled forward through the quagmire of desolation, picking his way as though familiar with every inch of ground, to the further corner where it was even darker, and where the noise of shunting freight trains drowned every other murmur of the night.

It was eight o'clock when Old Fags reached his room in Bolingbroke Buildings carrying his heavily laden sack across his shoulders. The child in Room 476 had been peevish and fretful all the afternoon and the two women were lying down exhausted. They heard Old Fags come in. He seemed very busy, banging about with bottles and tins and alternately coughing and wheezing. But soon the potent aroma of onions reached their nostrils and they knew he was preparing to keep his word.

At nine o'clock he staggered across with a steaming saucepan of hot stew. In contrast to the morning's conversation, which though devoid of self-consciousness, had taken on at times an air of moribund analysis, making little stabs at fundamental things, the evening passed off on a note of almost joyous levity. The stew was extremely good to the starving women, and Old Fags developed a vein of fantastic pleasantry. He talked unceasingly, sometimes on things they understood, sometimes on matters of which they were entirely ignorant and sometimes he appeared to them obtuse, maudlin and incoherent.

Nevertheless he brought to their room a certain light-hearted raillery that had never visited it before. No mention was made of Meads. The only blemish to the serenity of this bizarre supper party was that Old Fags developed intervals of violent coughing, intervals when he had to walk around the room and beat his chest. These fits had the unfortunate result of waking the baby. When this undesirable result had occurred for the fourth time Old Fags said:

"Oh, dear! Oh, dear! This won't do! Oh, no, this won't do. I must go back to my hotel!" a remark that caused paroxysms of mirth to old Mrs. Birdle.

Nevertheless, Old Fags retired and it was then just on eleven o'clock. The women went to bed, and all through the night Minnie heard the old man coughing. And while he is lying in this unfortunate condition let us follow the movements of Mr. Meads.

Meads jumped off the 'bus at Shepherd's Bush and hurried quickly in the direction that Old Fags had instructed him. He asked three people for the Pomeranian Road before an errand boy told him that he "believed it was somewhere off Giles Avenue," but at Giles Avenue no one seemed to know it. He retraced his steps in a very bad temper and enquired again. Five other people had never heard of it. So he went to a post office and a young lady in charge informed him that there was no such road in the neighbourhood.

He tried other roads whose names vaguely resembled it, then he came to the conclusion "that that blamed old fool had made a silly mistake." He took a 'bus back with a curious fear gnawing at the pit of his stomach, a fear that he kept thrusting back; he dare not allow himself to contemplate it. It was nearly seven thirty when he got back to Hyde Park and his eye quickly scanned the length of railing near which Old Fags was to be. Immediately that he saw no sign of him or the little dogs, a horrible feeling of physical sickness assailed him. The whole truth flashed through his mind. He saw the fabric of his life crumble to dust. He was conscious of visions of past acts and misdeeds tumbling over each other in a furious kaleidoscope.

The groom was terribly frightened. Mrs. Bastien Melland would be in at eight o'clock to dinner, and the first thing she would ask for would be the little dogs.

They were never supposed to go out after dark, but he had been busy that afternoon and arranged to take them out later. How was he to account for himself and their loss? He visualized himself in a dock, and all sorts of other horrid things coming up-a forged character, an affair in Norfolk and another at Enfield, and a little trouble with a bookmaker seven years ago. For he felt convinced that the dogs had gone for ever, and Old Fags with them.

He cursed blindly in his soul at his foul luck and the wretched inclination that had lured him to drink "beergin" with the old thief. Forms of terrific vengeance passed through his mind, if he should meet the old devil again. In the meantime what should he do? He had never even thought of making Old Fags give him any sort of address. He dared not go back to Hyde Park Square without the dogs. He ran breathlessly up and down peering in every direction. Eight o'clock came and there was still no sign! Suddenly he remembered Minnie Birdle. He remembered that the old ruffian had mentioned and seemed to know Minnie Birdle. It was a connection that he had hoped to have wiped out of his life, but the case was desperate.

Curiously enough, during his desultory courtship of Minnie he had never been to her home, but on the only occasion when he had visited it, after the birth of the child, he had done so under the influence of three pints of beer, and he hadn't the faintest recollection now of the number or the block. He hurried there, however, in feverish trepidation. Now Bolingbroke Buildings harbour some eight hundred people, and it is a remarkable fact that although the Birdles had lived there about a year, of the eleven people that Meads asked not one happened to know the name. People develop a profound sense of self-concentration in Bolingbroke Buildings. Meads wandered up all the stairs and through the slate tile passages. Twice he passed their door without knowing it: on the first occasion only five minutes after Old Fags had carried a saucepan of steaming stew from No. 475 to No. 476.

At ten o'clock he gave it up. He had four shillings on him and he adjourned to a small "pub" hard by and ordered a tankard of ale, and as an afterthought, three pennyworth of gin which he mixed in it. Probably he thought that this mixture, which was so directly responsible for the train of tragic circumstances that encompassed him, might continue to act in some manner towards a more desirable conclusion. It did indeed drive him to action of a sort, for he sat there drinking and smoking Navy Cut cigarettes, and by degrees he evolved a most engaging but impossible story of being lured to the river by three men and chloroformed, and when he came to, finding that the dogs and the men had gone.

He drank a further quantity of "beer-gin" and rehearsed his rôle in detail, and at length brought himself to the point of facing Mrs. Melland ....

It was the most terrifying ordeal of his life. The servants frightened him for a start. They almost shrieked when they saw him and drew back. Mrs. Bastien Melland had left word that he was to go to a breakfast-room in the basement directly he came in and she would see him.

There was a small dinner party on that evening and an agitated game of bridge. Meads had not stood on the hearthrug of the breakfast-room two minutes before he heard the foreboding swish of skirts, the door burst open and Mrs. Bastien Melland stood before him, a thing of penetrating perfumes, high-lights and trepidation.

She just said "Well!" and fixed her hard bright eyes on him. Meads launched forth into his improbable story, but he dared not look at her. He tried to gather together the pieces of the tale he had so carefully rehearsed in the "pub," but he felt like some helpless bark at the mercy of a hostile battle fleet, the searchlights of Mrs. Melland's cruel eyes were concentrated on him, while a flotilla of small diamonds on her heaving bosom winked and glittered with a dangerous insolence. He was stumbling over a phrase about the effects of chloroform when he became aware that Mrs. Melland was not listening to the matter of his story, she was only concerned with the manner.

Her lips were set and her straining eyes insisted on catching his. He looked full at her and caught his breath and stopped.

Mrs. Melland still staring at him was moving slowly to the door. A moment of panic seized him. He mumbled something and also moved towards the door. Mrs. Melland was first to grip the handle.

Meads made a wild dive and seized her wrist. But Mrs. Bastien-Melland came of a hard-riding Yorkshire family. She did not lose her head. She struck him across the mouth with her flat hand, and as he reeled back she opened the door and called to the servants. Suddenly Meads remembered that the rooms had a French window on to the garden. He pushed her clumsily against the door and sprang across the room. He clutched wildly at the bolts while Mrs. Melland's voice was ringing out:

"Catch that man! Hold him! Catch thief!" But before the other servants had had time to arrive he managed to get through the door and to pull it to after him. His hand was bleeding with cuts from broken glass but he leapt the wall and got into the shadow of some shrubs three gardens away. He heard whistles blowing and the dominant voice of Mrs. Melland directing a hue and cry. He rested some moments, then panic seized him and he laboured over another wall and found the passage of a semi-detached house. A servant opened a door and looked out and screamed. He struck her wildly and unreasonably on the shoulder and rushed up some steps and got into a front garden. There was no one there and he darted into the street and across the road.

In a few minutes he was lost in a labyrinth of back streets and laughing hysterically to himself. He had two shillings and eightpence on him. He spent fourpence of this on whisky, and then another fourpence just before the "pubs" closed. He struggled vainly to formulate some definite plan of campaign. The only point that seemed terribly clear to him was that he must get away. He knew

Mrs. Melland only too well. She would spare no trouble in hunting him down. She would exact the uttermost farthing. It meant gaol and ruin. The obvious impediment to getting away was that he had no money and no friends. He had not sufficient strength of character to face a tramp life. He had lived too long in the society of the pampered Pekinese. He loved comfort.

Out of the simmering tumult of his soul grew a very definite passion-the passion of hate. He developed a vast, bitter, scorching hatred for the person who had caused this ghastly climax to his unfortunate career-Old Fags. He went over the whole incidents of the day again, rapidly recalling every phase of Old Fags' conversation and manner. What a blind fool he was not to have seen through the filthy old swine's game! But what had he done with the dogs? Sold the lot for a pound, perhaps! The idea made Meads shiver. He slouched through the streets harbouring his pariah-like lust.

We will not attempt to record the psychologic changes that harassed the soul of Mr. Meads during the next two days and nights, the ugly passions that stirred him and beat their wings against the night, the tentative intuitions urging towards some vague new start, the various compromises he made with himself, his weakness and inconsistency that found him bereft of any quality other than the sombre shadow of some ill-conceived revenge. We will only note that on the evening of the day we mention he turned up at Bolingbroke Buildings. His face was haggard and drawn, his eyes blood-shot and his clothes tattered and muddy. His appearance and demeanour were unfortunately not so alien to the general character of Bolingbroke Buildings as to attract any particular attention, and he slunk like a wolf through the dreary passages and watched the people come and go.

It was at about a quarter to ten when he was going along a passage in Block "F" that he suddenly saw Minnie Birdie come out of one door and go into another.

His small eyes glittered and he went on tip-toe. He waited till Minnie was quite silent in her room and then he went stealthily to Room 475. He tried the handle and it gave. He opened the door and peered in. There was a cheap tin lamp guttering on a box that dimly revealed a room of repulsive wretchedness. The furniture seemed mostly to consist of bottles and rags. But in one corner on a mattress he beheld the grinning face of his enemy- Old Fags. Meads shut the door silently and stood with his back to it.

"Oh!" he said. "So here we are at last, old bird, eh!" This move was apparently a supremely successful dramatic coup, for Old Fags lay still, paralyzed with fear, no doubt.

"So this is our little 'ome, eh?" he continued," where we bring little dogs and sell 'em. What have you got to say, you old" The groom's face blazed into a sudden accumulated fury. He thrust his chin forward and let forth a volley of frightful and blasting oaths. But Old Fags didn't answer; his shiny face seemed to be intensely amused with this outburst.

"We got to settle our little account, old bird, see?" and the suppressed fury of his voice denoted some physical climax. "Why the hell don't you answer?" he suddenly shrieked, and springing forward he lashed Old Fags across the cheek.

And then a terrible horror came over him. The cheek he had struck was as cold as marble and the head fell a little impotently to one side. Trembling, as though struck with an ague, the groom picked up the guttering lamp and held it close to the face of Old Fags. It was set in an impenetrable repose, the significance of which even the groom could not misunderstand. The features were calm and childlike, lit by a half smile of splendid tolerance that seemed to have overridden the temporary buffets of a queer world. Meads had no idea how long he stood there gazing horror-struck at the face of his enemy. He only knew that he was presently conscious that Minnie Birdle was standing by his side and as he looked at her, her gaze was fixed on Old Fags and a tear was trickling down either cheek.

"'E's dead," she said. "Old Fags is dead. 'E died this morning of noomonyer." She said this quite simply as though it was a statement that explained the wonder of her presence. She did not look at Meads or seem aware of him. He watched the flickering light from the lamp illumining the underside of her chin and nostrils and her quivering brows.

"'E's dead," she said again, and the statement seemed to come as an edict of dismissal as though love and hatred and revenge had no place in these fundamental things.

Meads looked from her to the tousled head leaning slightly to one side of the mattress and he felt himself in the presence of forces he could not comprehend. He put the lamp back quietly on the box and tip-toed from the room.

Out once more in the night, his breath came quickly and a certain buoyancy drove him on. He dared not contemplate the terror of that threshold upon which he had almost trodden. He only knew that out of the surging maelstrom of irresolution some fate had gripped him. He walked with a certain elasticity in the direction of Millwall.

There would be doss-houses and docks there and many a good ship that glided forth to strange lands, carrying human freight of whom few questions would be asked, for the ship wanted them to ease her way through the regenerating seas ....

And in the cold hours of the early dawn Minnie Birdle lay awake listening to the rhythmic breathing of her child.

And she thought of that strange old man, less terrible now in his mask of death than when she had first known him.

No one to-morrow would follow to his pauper's grave, and yet at one time who knows? She dared not speculate upon the tangled skein of this difficult life that had brought him to this. She only knew that somehow from it she had drawn a certain vibrant force that made her build a monster resolution. Her child! She would be strong, she would throw her frail body between it and the shafts of an unthinking world. She leant across it, listening intensely, then kissed the delicate down upon its skull, crooning with animal satisfaction at the smell of its warm soft flesh.

Stacy Aumonier – A Short Biography

Stacy Aumonier was born at Hampstead Road near Regent's Park, London on 31st March 1877.

He came from a family with a strong and sustained tradition in the visual arts; sculptors and painters.

In 1890 the teenage Aumonier attended Cranleigh School in Surrey. Although he would later write critically about English public schools (with articles for the London Evening Standard and New York Times) in how they tried to impose conformity on students, records indicate that he integrated well into Cranleigh. Aumonier was a passionate cricket player, belonged to the Literary and Debating Society, and, in his final year, became a prefect.

On leaving school it seemed the family tradition of the visual arts would be his career path. In particular his early talents were that of a landscape painter. He exhibited paintings at the Royal Academy in 1902 and 1903, and 1908. An exhibition of his work would later be held at the Goupil Gallery in London in 1911.

In 1907 he married the international concert pianist, Gertrude Peppercorn, at West Horsley in Surrey. She herself was the daughter of a landscape painter (Arthur Douglas Peppercorn, occasionally cited as 'the English Corot'.) A son, Timothy, was born in 1921.

A year after his marriage, Aumonier began a brief career in a second branch of the arts at which he enjoyed outstanding success—as a stage performer writing and performing his own sketches.

The Observer newspaper commented that "...the stage lost in him a real and rare genius, he could walk out alone before any audience, from the simplest to the most sophisticated, and make it laugh or cry at will."

In 1915, Aumonier published a short story 'The Friends' which was well received (and voted one of the best short stories of 1915 by the Boston Magazine, Transcript).

Despite his age being 40 in 1917 he was called up for service in World War I. He began as a private in the Army Pay Corps, and then transferred as a draughtsman in the Ministry of National Service.

By now he had four books published—two novels and two books of short stories—and his occupation is recorded with the Army Medical Board as 'author.'

In the mid-1920s, Aumonier received the shattering diagnosis that he had contracted tuberculosis. In the last few years of his life, he would spend long spells in various sanatoria, some better than others. In a letter to his friend, Rebecca West, written shortly before his death, he described the debilitating conditions in a sanatorium in Norfolk during the winter of 1927, where the dampness was so severe that a newspaper left beside the bed would feel "sodden to the touch in the morning."

Shortly before his death, Stacy Aumonier sought treatment in Switzerland, but died of the disease in Clinique La Prairie at Clarens beside Lake Geneva on 21st December 1928. He was 55.

Whilst Aumonier's works are now slowly coming back into circulation at the time of his death his works were extremely popular and his loss was a profound tragedy for literary society.

The chief fiction critic of The Observer, Gerald Gould wrote: "His gifts were almost fantastically various; they embraced all the arts; but it was the charm and generosity of his personality which made him—what he unquestionably was—one of the most popular men of his generation." It went on: "The things he wrote will be remembered when the company of his friends (no man had more friends, or more devoted and admiring) are with him in the grave; but just now, to those who knew him, the thing most vividly present is the charm and wisdom of the man they knew."

Of his general appearance and manner Gerald Cumberland gives us this interesting set of observations: "A distinguished man, this—distinguished both in mind and appearance. Self-conscious. Perhaps. Why not? His hair is worn a trifle long, and it is arranged so that his fine forehead, broad and high, may be fully revealed. Round his neck is a very high collar and a modern stock. When in repose, his face has a look of shy eagerness; his quick eyes glance here and there gathering a thousand impressions to be stored up in his brain. It is the face of a man extremely sensitive to external stimulus; one feels that his brain works not only rapidly, but with great accuracy. And at heart, he takes himself and his work seriously, though he likes on occasion to pretend that he is only a philanderer."

In literary terms Aumonier was amongst the best short story writers these shores have produced.

The Nobel Prize winning author John Galsworthy called him "A real master of the short story. The first essential in a short-story writer is the power of interesting sentence by sentence. Aumonier had this power in prime degree. You do not have to 'get into' his stories. He is especially notable for investing his figures with the breadth of life within a few sentences." Galsworthy asserted that Aumonier "is never heavy, never boring, never really trivial; interested himself, he keeps us interested. At the back of his tales, there is belief in life and a philosophy of life, and of how many short story writers can that be said? ...He follows no fashion and no school. He is always himself. And can't he write? Ah! Far better than far more pretentious writers. Nothing escapes his eye, but he describes without affectation or redundancy, and you sense in him a feeling for beauty that is never obtruded. He gets values right, and that is to say nearly everything. The easeful fidelity of his style has militated against his reputation in these somewhat posturing times. But his shade may rest in peace, for in this volume, at least he will outlive nearly all the writers of his day." In summing his up Galsworthy suggested that, through his stories, he would "outlive all the writers of his day."

James Hilton (author of Goodbye, Mr Chips and Lost Horizon) said "I think his very best works ought to be included in any anthology of the best short stories ever written." He cited 'The Octave of Jealously' as his favourite short story for the March 1939 edition of Good Housekeeping saying it was a "bitterly brilliant tale."

Rebecca West said of his writing in 1922 that his ability to blend reality with the imaginary was "the envy of all artists."

Stacy Aumonier -- A Concise Bibliography

More than 87 short stories in more than 25 magazines, and in 6 volumes published during Aumonier's lifetime.

Among more than 20 other magazines, his work appeared in Argosy Magazine, John O' London's Weekly, The Strand Magazine and The Saturday Evening Post, as well as being anthologized, and adapted for film and television.

Short Story Collections

The Golden Windmill & Other Stories (1921)
The Friends & Other Stories (1917)
Miss Bracegirdle & Other Stories (1923)

Novels

Olga Bardel (1916)

Three Bars Interval (1917)
Just Outside (1917)
The Querrils (1919)
One After Another (1920)
Heartbeat (1922)

Other Works

A volume of 14 Character Studies: Odd Fish (1923)

A volume of 15 Essays: Essays of Today and Yesterday (1926)

Printed in the USA
CPSIA information can be obtained
at www.ICGtesting.com
LVHW021240091223
766101LV00011B/986